LISTENER'S FOLLY

Beverley Gordon was delighted when she was offered the job of cataloguing a library in a Westmorland country house by Bruce Sheavyn. Life at Willerton Grange proved to be a very different proposition from existence in a hostel bed-sitter, but Beverley soon discovered that even here life had its problems. At the very outset of her stay there she overheard the words 'I will kill him myself', and though she succeeded in convincing herself that the words had not the sinister meaning she first imputed to them, a series of 'accidents' faced her with a new problem. How can one tell a man that his wife is a potential murderer?

Listener's Folly

Norah Whittle

A Seymour Book

CHIVERS PRESS
BATH

First published 1968
by
Hurst & Blackett Ltd
This Large Print edition published by
Chivers Press
by arrangement with the author
1981

ISBN 0 85119 418 4

British Library Cataloguing in Publication Data

Whittle, Norah
    Listener's folly.—Large print ed.
    I. Title
    823'.9'1F

    ISBN 0–85119–418–4

Photoset, printed and bound
in Great Britain by
REDWOOD BURN LIMITED
Trowbridge & Esher

CHAPTER ONE

'I hate men.' Beverley Gordon flung her handbag on the bed and flopped into the semi-easy chair which, with its opposite number—already occupied by the girl with whom she shared the room—constituted the main claim for the hyphened 'sitting' to what might more aptly have been termed a bedroom. The only other objects of furniture which were not of a definitely bedroom nature were the two small, shabby, oak desks, and, perhaps, the old-fashioned gas fire whose discoloured elements now stared vacantly into the room. 'Prhh!' Beverley rubbed her hands. 'Why haven't you lit Grandpa?'

'No shillings, and it isn't worth it anyhow.' Sandra had christened the gas fire 'Grandpa' because of its incurable habit of spluttering and burping in its efforts to digest the shillings which it swallowed so voraciously. 'Just like Grandpa,' she had said. 'What's the trouble with men now?' she asked, peering up at the other girl through the curtain of fair hair which was nearly as efficient a sight restrictor as a horse's blinkers—but Sandra could, and did, toss hers aside if she felt the occasion warranted it. The sight, and sound, of

1

Beverley inveighing against the opposite sex was too mundane to merit this treatment. She merely peered through the strands.

'Oh, the usual. It's Colin Watmough. He just can't keep his hands off me. It isn't as though I gave him any encouragement. I don't.'

'I can believe you.' Sandra laughed. It must have been the attraction of the opposites which was responsible for the close friendship which existed between the two girls, and had done so ever since the first day when they had met as two shy little first-formers at Brompton Comprehensive School. Sandra had consciously, even in those early days, spread her honey to entice the wavering male. Wherever Sandra was, unless Beverley was with her, there was always a cluster of admirers, a cluster which, as time went on, became whittled down to one or two, though the one or two formed part of a constantly changing pattern. Sandra had no intention of settling down to one particular partner until she had made a complete survey of the matrimonial market.

It was because Beverley Gordon was so different from their own daughter that Sandra's parents had acceded to her demands that she should be allowed to join her friend when Beverley took a secretarial post in

2

London. Mr. and Mrs. Knight were well aware that, whereas their daughter had always responded with open arms to the questing male, her friend had been equally constant in her rebuffs and studious aloofness. As friends, fellow students, she had welcomed them but, to the first physical contact, the slightest hint of sexual interest, her response was akin to that of the anemone—she closed up completely. It was not surprising that her friend was more than ready to believe that Colin Watmough had received no encouragement.

'The trouble with you, Beverley, is that you are taking so long to grow up.'

'I'm not.' Beverley rebutted the charge indignantly. 'I'm a lot more grown up than you are.' This was true in many ways. Beverley Gordon was far more responsible, far less scatterbrained than her friend, and also much more serious-minded. Life had made her so. Sandra was the only girl, and the youngest child, of a prosperous, middle-class couple. It was difficult to say who had spoiled her most, her parents or her brothers—she had been, and still was, the darling of the family. Beverley was the only child of a mother whose means of support apart from her own exertions had been negligible. She had died two years ago. It was only natural that Beverley should feel Sandra's outlook on life to be immature, that she regarded her escapades with the tolerance one would extend to a loved puppy. Sandra, however, had a different view as to what was implied by the process of growing up.

'You don't even know the facts of life.' She silenced the indignant protest. 'Oh, yes, in theory, but I was more grown-up at fifteen than you are now. I knew everything when I was fifteen.' She spread her arms in token of an all-embracing knowledge. 'Oh, you can grin,' she said petulantly, 'but you know what I mean.' She became serious. 'You know, Beverley, you are going to be badly hurt some day. When you do fall in love, you'll get it very badly and you won't know how to cope. My way's much the best.'

'I'm not going to fall in love,' the other girl pronounced with all the arrogance of an untried twenty-year-old. 'I've just told you I hate men. At least young ones.'

'You know, your father did you a very bad turn when he ran away.' Sandra eyed her friend narrowly. 'I don't just mean by depriving you of a parent. That's bad enough, of course, but what I mean is that he has poisoned your view of men in general. I'm sure it's because of that you are so queer about them.'

4

'I'm no . . .' began Beverley, then stopped. She was aware that she was merely being contrary. She knew only too well that there was something lacking in her, that—by the yardstick of her companions—she was not completely normal. She had never hitherto aligned that abnormality with her father's defection. 'It might be,' she conceded slowly.

'I'm sure it is.' Sandra Knight prided herself on her knowledge of human nature. Her psychology might be amateurish, it was certainly home-spun, but it was vastly in advance of her companion's. 'If my father had left my mother when I was seven should I have been different?'

'You most certainly would.' Even Beverley's fore-shortened knowledge of human nature allowed her that deduction.

'I mean, should I have been different in the same way as you are? Of course I should have been different, but would I have been like you, and not liked men?'

'I can't imagine it,' laughed Beverley. It was as impossible to visualise Sandra without her swains as to imagine a tree without its branches. Sandra laughed.

'No, I don't suppose so, but I still think it is your father's fault that you are like that.'

'Well, what am I to do about it?' demanded the other girl.

'Write to Evelyn Home.' She threw aside the magazine which she had been reading when Beverley entered the room. 'But, seriously, you are going to have to face up to it some day. It isn't as though you are one of those unattractive girls with pudding faces and thick ankles. You're frightfully attractive really. The boys at school used to rave about you. You've got everything—a perfect figure, none of my curves and bulges,' she looked down disparagingly at her own pleasing, if slightly over-plump, body, 'good features, glorious hair. You never have to spend your time and money on perms, but you might let it grow a bit,' she added, 'then it would be heavenly. As it is you look a bit too much like a boy.'

'I sometimes wish I was a boy. Then I would not have all this trouble,' Beverley offered gloomily.

'You would have others.' Sandra jumped up suddenly. 'Bags I have first bath. I'm going out with Laurie tonight.'

Baths at the hostel were hardly come by. It was practically impossible to get one at night. The two girls had developed the routine of taking theirs between the return from the office and dinner. As Beverley busied herself in the bedroom, waiting her turn in the bathroom, she meditated on the recent

6

conversation. The more she thought about it, the more convinced she became that her unnatural dislike of men—she was quite prepared to admit that it was unnatural— stemmed from her father's behaviour, not just from the behaviour itself but from its impact on his wife. She concluded that it was this which had given that bitter twist to her mother's nature, which was responsible for her scorn of men and of sex.

'Don't be taken in by their fair words,' her mother had told her. 'They will promise you the earth to get what they want and once they have got it they no longer want it.'

Beverley had always taken her mother's attitude for granted. She had always believed that the fault had all been on her father's side. Now she began to wonder whether he had not had much to put up with before he took the final step. Was this because she had started to grow up? It had taken her all these years to realise that to this problem, as to most, there might be a second side. She knew nothing of her father's movements since he had left his home apart from the fact that he had married again, emigrated to Australia, and had another family. According to her mother, the allowance he made to her was a mere pittance and even that had ceased three years ago. Word had come then, of his death and the

7

consequent cessation of the payments.

Early memories of her father flocked into her mind, memories which had lain dormant for years, forced into the background by her mother's bitterness against him. She saw him now, playing with her, remembered her sense of loss when she had been told that she had no 'Daddy' now, that he was not a good daddy. And she remembered how, before that time the brightness in her life had stemmed from her father, that there had always been an aura of discontent about her mother. Had it in those days been caused by her husband's behaviour or had it been part of her mother's character?

Beverley shrugged her shoulders. That was a question which could never be answered. What she did know was that after her father's death, life had been a still greater struggle for her mother. It was then that it was decided that a university course was out of the question for her, that she must be content with a secretarial training. She had not yet finished that when her mother died.

It was only during that last illness, mercifully short, that the girl had discovered that her mother had been struggling against ill-health for several years. She had never actually complained, but had Beverley been older and wiser, she would probably have realised that the pessimism and short temper which she had so often resented were the only outlet which a sick woman allowed herself. She had loved her mother, but the relationship between them had been increasingly marred by the older woman's constant fault-finding and lack of understanding. The girl's sense of grievance was heightened by the knowledge that she indulged in none of the teenage extravagances which characterised the behaviour of many of her contemporaries. She often felt that she had been too biddable.

'You ought to kick over the traces a bit,' Sandra had told her. Sandra was on excellent terms with both her parents in spite of many lapses from grace.

As soon as her course was completed, Beverley applied for, and obtained, a secretarial post in a London business firm. Sandra clamoured to do likewise. She, also, had foresworn a university career—much to the annoyance of the staff, for Sandra, in spite of her surface frivolity, was an able French scholar. Beverley's defection had been regretted, but her mother's visit to the headmaster had convinced him of its necessity. There was no such reason in Sandra's case.

'What's the use of spending all my youth swotting?' she had said. 'I'm going to get married and I might as well enjoy myself until I do.' And enjoy herself she did. The only fly in the ointment, and that went for Beverley too, was that the two girls had not got their own flat, but permission to go to London had only been granted to Sandra on the condition that she lived in a hostel until she was twenty-one. Then she could please herself.

'All yours!' Sandra was back in the bedroom, her round face pink and shining, her fair hair hidden under a blue scarf, wrapped turban-like round her head. 'I've left the bath salts on the ledge. Don't forget to bring them back or they'll be snaffled.'

The bathroom was damp and steam-filled, reeking of the scented bath salts which Sandra had obviously scattered with an over-lavish hand. The other girl's first reaction to this already saturated atmosphere was, as always, one of slight annoyance—it was something she had never experienced at home—but the annoyance was quickly swallowed up in the sensuous bliss of her own immersion in the deep water; the notice demanding that the water be not more than five inches deep might never have been. Conscience might have prompted attention to it had the hour been later, but at this time the notice was made to be ignored. She lay and wallowed. No hippopotamus in its mud bath could, she thought, have been more content. All those troubling thoughts which had so obsessed her a few moments ago were washed away. The hot, scented water lapped her in a euphoria which accompanied her out of the bath, through the process of drying, back into the drab bed-cum-sitting-room. It was Sandra who unwound the cocoon in which she had wrapped herself, who impaled her on the pin of self-criticism and doubt.

'You know you really ought to take yourself in hand about this "boy business". It's no good thinking that with your looks you are not going to have men running after you.' Her eyes raked the other girl from top to toe, from her small head crowned with crisply waving short brown hair, past the slim, almost sexless body—she was still in the state of dressing where she wore nothing but bra and panties—to the long slim legs. She, herself, was already dressed for the evening. Her bright green, mini-length sheath dress accentuated every curve. She looked fresh, attractive, very young, very feminine.

'Why must they always start to maul you?' the other girl asked indignantly. 'I thought Colin was quite nice and sensible until today. Then he started.' She shuddered as she thought of the young man's questing hands.

'Oh, well, forget it. I bet you settled Master

11

Colin all right.'

'Yes,' but Beverley did not say that Colin was not the only trouble at the office. Mr. Pemberton, the partner whose particular secretary she was, had lately shown amatory signs.

'Well, that's O.K. then. I think . . .'

Whatever she thought was lost for at that moment the dinner gong went. As it was a case of first down, first served, and Beverley was still in a state of undress, the next few minutes were spent by both girls in a feverish effort to get Beverley into the dining-room fully clothed before the depredations of the invading horde had reduced the chances of a decent meal to nil. The girls were both young and healthy with appetites to correspond, and the hostel authorities were decidedly niggardly in their catering.

Sandra's words bore fruit. When Colin Watmough, two days later, asked Beverley to go out with him—the brush-off had not been as final as she had thought—she agreed. Sandra greeted her decision with approval.

'And if he wants to kiss you, let him,' she admonished. 'It's not such a terrible ordeal to be kissed by a fellow.' She giggled. 'In fact, it's not terrible at all. It's really rather nice. Usually.'

'It may be for you. We are obviously made

12

differently.'

'Bosh! What's that Kipling thing about somebody O'Grady and the colonel's lady? I can't remember what it was exactly, but I guess Kipling had got something there. Anyhow, you act like somebody O'Grady and not the colonel's lady tonight.'

'I'll try.' Beverley laughed. Sandra's nonsense did much to banish the misgivings which had assailed her as she dressed for this date with Colin. Sandra, herself, was again going out with Laurie. Beverley had begun to wonder if her friend's straying fancies had at last become anchored. Laurie Henderson had had a longer innings than any other previous admirer. It looked as though he might carry his bat through to the end.

'Will I do?' She presented herself for her friend's approval. Her new winter coat, cherry-coloured with a black velvet collar, was being worn for the first time.

'Yes, you look smashing.' Sandra looked admiringly at the little black fur hat perched on the brown curls. 'Colin ought to feel honoured. Fancy you wearing a hat.'

'Do you like it?' It was so rarely that Beverley wore a hat—she was blessed with the sort of hair which was on good terms with any type of weather—that when she did, she felt over-dressed.

'Yes,' said Sandra again. 'I told you, you look smashing. Now, off you go and enjoy yourself.' She gave the other girl a push towards the door. 'I won't say "don't do anything that I wouldn't".' She chuckled. 'What I say is, "do what I would do".'

The evening passed off pleasantly, almost tamely. Beverley discovered that all her heart-searchings, all her brave intentions, all Sandra's exhortations, had been superfluous. She came to the conclusion that her earlier treatment of his attentions must have had an effect for Colin behaved most circumspectly. Even the darkness of the cinema did not loosen him up. He made no attempt to get closer to her, did not even try to hold her hand, and when they finally reached the hostel his pleasant farewell was as formal as though it had been made under the eyes of a dancing teacher. Beverley's feelings as she went up to her room bordered on the anti-climax. Suddenly the funny side struck her. She was still laughing when Sandra entered the room. She must have followed almost immediately on Beverley's heels.

'What's the joke?' demanded the other girl. 'How did it go?' she asked almost in the same breath. 'Did you let him kiss you good night?'

'He didn't try to.' Beverley stopped laughing. It did not seem so funny now. She

14

was annoyed at the note of apology which had crept into her voice. It was as though she was ashamed.

'Oh!' The single syllable dropped expressively into the momentary silence which followed her statement. 'I suppose you had squashed him so effectively the other day that he dared not try anything. He'll probably be different next time. If there is a next time,' she said suddenly. 'Did he ask you to go out again?'

'Yes.' Sandra gave a sigh of relief. 'He asked me to go tomorrow night, but I can't. I've got to work late. Mr. Pemberton told me this afternoon that he wanted me to stay late tomorrow.'

'That's a new departure for him, isn't it?'

'Yes. I've promised Colin that I will go to the ballet with him on Saturday.'

She did not want Sandra to embroider on the theme of the newness of Mr. Pemberton's demands, nor did she want to tell her how she dreaded her late session, dreaded the thought of being alone in the office building with her employer. She was well aware that in all probability there would be no one else in the building. Even the liftman went off duty at six o'clock. She knew that because she had once worked late for Mr. Westmacott, the senior partner, when his own secretary had been

15

away ill. She had not minded that at all, but there had been tiny episodes lately which had made her chary of being alone with her own boss. Tomorrow evening she would be alone with him with a vengeance.

'What on earth have you hunted out that jumper for? I thought you said you were going to give it to a jumble sale.' Those were the words which Sandra hurled at her the next morning as she was pulling the grey jumper over her head. It had been a bad buy. She had only worn it once or twice, realising that it did less than nothing for her. It was for that very reason that she was wearing it today. The less attractive she looked this evening the safer she would feel.

'Oh, I just thought I would give it a turn.' She tried to infuse a convincing note of nonchalance into the tone.

'Are you feeling like sackcloth and ashes after your night out with Colin? I thought you said nothing happened.'

'It didn't, and I'm not wearing sackcloth and ashes for Colin.' She might have added that she was wearing them for Mr. Pemberton, but she did not.

For once the day passed all too quickly. She became a clock-watcher, not because she wanted the fingers to move more quickly, but because she wanted to stay their motion, to

16

make them move more slowly so that the dreaded time when she would be alone with Mr. Pemberton might be pushed off as long as possible. It was in vain that she told herself that she was being foolish, that her employer was too much of a gentleman to take advantage of the position and to make unwelcome advances. And, if by any chance, he did appear to be becoming over-friendly, she was sufficiently adept at being frigid to be able to put a stop to it. Look at Colin last night. So she admonished herself throughout the day; nevertheless she felt like a trapped animal when the door finally closed on the last of her colleagues. She knocked on the door of Mr. Pemberton's private office.

'Are you ready for me, Mr. Pemberton?' she asked.

'Just a moment, Beverley. Sit down until I have finished this.'

Why am I so afraid of this man? she wondered, as she watched him working at his desk. He certainly did not look the villain she was imagining him to be. He was just a typical, well-dressed business man. His mousy hair was brushed back from a high forehead, which, combined with the horn-rimmed glasses and the spare frame, made him look more intellectual than he really was.

'Well, do I pass?'

Beverley blushed. She had not meant to stare. She drew her chair closer to the desk as the man pushed his papers away and prepared to dictate. For the next two hours they worked steadily, the only interruption being that caused by the entry of the liftman.

'I'm going now, sir.' He put the bunch of keys on the table.

'All right, George. I'll lock up.'

Beverley felt a slight tremor pass through her as she heard the bang of the outer door, but any trepidation she might have felt could not find house room when it had to compete with the work in hand. That needed all her powers of concentration. Ronald Pemberton was no mean taskmaster.

'Good, that will do! We've done a jolly good evening's work.' The man opened a drawer in his desk and pushed his papers into it. Beverley sat up and straightened her back. For the last half-hour she had felt that if she had to hold her present position much longer her back would break in two, not to mention the fact that her fingers were beginning to become as wooden as the pencil which they held, and her brain threatened to strike, to refuse to translate Mr. Pemberton's flowing words into the requisite symbols. 'You've got plenty of work to carry on with tomorrow,' the voice went on, but luckily its contents need

18

not be transferred to paper now. 'I shan't be in the office tomorrow: I have to go up north, but I will be in on Friday.'

Beverley rose; she stretched her stiffened limbs and was about to turn towards the door when Ronald Pemberton, swivelling round in his chair, stretched out his hand and pulled her towards him.

'You're a pretty girl, Beverley.' Before she knew what was happening he had pulled her on to his knee.

'Mr. Pemberton, let me go!' She struggled to release herself, but the man tightened his hold on her. Pushing her back, he held her tightly with one arm while the other hand explored under her tight grey skirt.

'Don't pretend you are not enjoying it,' he said as he pressed his lips on hers, forcing his tongue between her lips.

Beverley jerked her head furiously, managing to break the contact between their lips, but she could not free herself from his grip.

'Don't be a fool, girl,' he said. 'Don't play hard to get.' He looked at her half angrily, half amusedly. 'You need not try to pretend that a girl with your looks is new to this.' Beverley continued to struggle, tried, in vain, to bite the hand which held her. 'If you don't behave, I'll put you across my knee the other way,' he

19

said, 'and see how you like that.' He made as though to carry out his threat.

The slight movement gave the girl her opportunity. She wriggled herself free from his grasp, tumbling on the floor as she did so.

She was up like a flash of lightning. Anger, disgust, humiliation, one or all of them, transformed her from her usual law-abiding self into an avenging fury. In the one second before she struck him, Ronald Pemberton had time to tell himself that she looked marvellous, a prize well worth taming, but the thought was short-lived. The girl's hand met his face with a fierceness which sent his spectacles flying to the furthest corner of the room.

CHAPTER TWO

What had she done? Beverley stood aghast. The sudden impact of her hand with her employer's face, the sight of the flying spectacles, the sound of splintering glass, jerked her into a realisation of what she had done. Her natural self began to reassert itself.

'I'm sorry...' she began, but her employer's face as he rose from his chair checked the words. She was not only not sorry, she was not going to stay in the same room as this man for another minute. She caught sight of the bunch of keys lying on the desk. Snatching them up she rushed out of the room, down the stairs, to the front door. Her fingers trembled as she tried to fit one key after another into the lock. She looked fearfully up the stairs, expecting to see Mr. Pemberton in pursuit, but there was no sign of him, nor yet any sound from the room from which she had just fled. Though she did not know it, Ronald Pemberton was already telling himself that he had acted like a fool, and wondering what would be his attitude when he next saw his secretary. It was a good job there was a long weekend in between. It would give them both time to recover.

At last Beverley found the key which fitted. Leaving the key in the lock she pulled open the heavy door and stepped out on to the pavement. Pulling the door to behind her she began to run as though she were being pursued, but not for many minutes. The glances of the passers-by told her that she was attracting attention. She forced herself into a walk. It was not until she reached her own square that she allowed her feelings to take charge again. She burst into the bedroom where Sandra was busy applying the final touch of lipstick before going down to dinner.

'Hello, you are early, aren't you?' She turned. 'What's the matter, Beverley? What's happened?'

'Mr. Pem . . .' Beverley was unable to get further. She collapsed into a chair and sobbed and sobbed.

'What's the matter?' asked Sandra again. 'What about Mr. Pemberton?' She knelt down by the chair, trying to comfort the other girl. 'He hasn't given you the sack, has he?' She could not imagine such a thing having happened—Beverley was far too good a secretary to be sacked—but neither could she think of any other reason to account for her friend's intense distress.

'N-no.' Beverley shook her head. 'He . . .' She shuddered, the sobs, which had lessened

22

for a moment, took charge again. Sandra, realising the futility of expecting an answer at this stage, continued to kneel by her, stroking her hands, uttering little clucking sounds which were meant to be comforting.

'Y-you'll miss your dinner.' Beverley had recovered sufficiently to know that there were other people in the world beside herself and Ronald Pemberton.

'It doesn't matter. I'll get Laurie to take me somewhere later. Or would you like me to phone him and tell him I can't go out tonight? Would you like me to stay in with you?'

'No, I will be all right. You go and get your dinner.'

Sandra stood deliberating. It was obvious that Beverley was not yet in a fit state to explain what had happened to upset her so much. Possibly in half an hour's time she would be sufficiently recovered to not only tell her story but to profit from her friend's attempts at comfort.

'All right,' she said, 'but I will come straight upstairs after. What about your dinner? You asked them to save some, didn't you?'

'Yes, but I don't want any.' She felt that the very sight of food would make her sick.

'I'll see if I can get anything nice and light from the kitchen,' Sandra promised. 'Well, I'll be seeing you.' She tried to hide her real

23

concern. The sight of the usually stoical Beverley in such distress disturbed her more than she cared to acknowledge.

Left to herself, Beverley started on the road back to the sanity which had almost deserted her. She had stopped crying now and lay slumped in her chair, staring vacantly into space, her mind washed clear of consecutive thought, her feelings—for the moment— numb. The horror of her recent experience still lay very near the surface, the knowledge that the consequences of that experience were crying out to be dealt with lurked just round the periphery of her thoughts, but the shock, followed as it had been by the bout of tears, had, for the time being, drained her of the will to think, the power to feel. When the door opened to re-admit Sandra she was not only comparatively calm, she had begun to think of the immediate future.

'Hello, feeling better? Look what I've got.' Sandra pushed the door to with her foot, her hands were otherwise engaged in holding a tray. 'I told them a sob tale in the kitchen, said you were feeling rotten—quite true—and could they rustle up something really light and tempting for you. I put on all my charm and look what they've come up with. Mushroom soup and a luscious-looking caramel cream! I bet that's what old Horsfall was having for dinner.' Miss Horsfall was the hostel warden. Sandra plumped the tray down on one of the beds and then turned to Beverley. 'Now, just get that into you while I'm getting ready to go out and then we'll talk. I'll phone Laurie to tell him I'll be a bit late.'

To her surprise Beverley found that she was not only able to eat the food, she was able to enjoy it. 'Thank you, Sandra, that was good. I feel better for it.'

'You've finished it all?' Sandra looked at the tray, with its empty dishes. 'Fine! I'll take the tray down and then phone Laurie. I won't be two ticks.'

The two ticks stretched out to ten minutes, but it could hardly be expected that a telephone conversation between Sandra and one of her boy-friends could be anything but a lengthy business even though she might be seeing him that same evening.

'There, I've settled that. I've told Laurie I can't meet him until nine o'clock. Now tell me what your Mr. Pemberton has been up to to get you in such a tizzie.' She pulled the other easy chair up to her friend's and prepared to listen.

The telling proved no easy task. Beverley's innate fastidiousness bungled at the details, but, prompted by her more worldly-wise friend, she succeeded eventually in giving an

25

unexpurgated account of Ronald Pemberton's conduct.

'I'm not going back to the office. I can't,' she said passionately when she came to the end of her own tale, of Sandra's questions.

'But you must.' Sandra stared at her in dismay. 'You can't just leave like that without giving notice. You wouldn't get a reference and you would find it almost impossible to get another job without one. Any employer would want to know what you had been doing all this time since you left school.'

'I can't help that. I'm not going back to work for that man.' Beverley shuddered. She was reliving the few short minutes which had filled her with such horror. Would she ever feel clean again? she wondered, but even as the thought passed through her mind she knew that she was over-dramatising, that though it was an experience which was etched indelibly on her mind, the sense of uncleanness with which it smeared her was only transitory.

'You have got to.' Sandra was firm. Her surface frivolity was rooted in common sense. 'You can't live on love. You have got to get another job—if you feel you can't stay there, and I can quite see that—but you have got to work out your notice.'

'How can I go back to that man?' appealed the other girl. 'I should never feel safe with him, apart from the fact that I could not bear to look him in the face again.'

'He probably feels that way himself,' Sandra mused. 'I don't expect he is any more anxious to see you again than you are to see him.'

'Well then!' said Beverley triumphantly.

'Didn't you say he was not going to be in the office tomorrow?'

'Yes.' Beverley brightened. She had forgotten that. At least there was no reason why she should not go to the office tomorrow.

'Good! That means you can go tomorrow and I've just had an idea. Couldn't you ask the senior partner, Mr. Westmacott—isn't it?—to put you in the typing pool for the last week?'

'I suppose I could. Yes, Sandra, I will serve out my notice. But I won't stay a moment longer,' she said fiercely.

'Nobody is asking you to, so pipe down. Anyhow I had better be off or Laurie will be standing me up next.' She went to the mirror to replenish her lipstick. 'But you had better grow a second skin, Beverley,' she advised. 'You know, you can't go through life changing your job every time the boss makes a pass at you. You are sure to get it. You are too pretty not to and men are like that. The trouble with you is that you are too innocent. But I must fly. Good-bye.'

'Too innocent!' The door had closed behind the other girl. Beverley spoke to the empty room. She did not feel innocent, not after tonight, but also she did not feel any more capable of coping with a similar experience should it come her way again. What was she going to do?

The next morning found her still determined to give in her notice. As she looked regretfully round her little office—it was only six months since she had been promoted to her own office—she thought how she was going to miss it. There were so many little touches which made it hers and hers alone—the desk calendar which Sandra had given her, her mother's photograph, her little travelling clock, the pottery vase which she had bought when she had gone to Stratford for a holiday. That sometimes sported a few flowers, but today it was empty—London flowers were too expensive, too much of a luxury to be indulged in regularly. After today this would no longer be hers. She had been happy here, and loved her little sanctum. She shook herself impatiently. It was no use harbouring regrets now. She had definitely made up her mind and had no intention of changing it. Nor did she want to. This office and Mr. Pemberton were bound together. She could not have the one without the other and she most certainly wanted to have nothing more to do with Mr. Pemberton.

She put her bag down on her desk. There was plenty of work for her to do today. There was no time to waste in needless repinings. She wondered what had happened to the papers she had prepared last night. She had rushed out of that other office last night with no thought of the hours of work which had led up to the devastating finale. Would the papers be on Mr. Pemberton's desk? She went through to the other room. It needed quite an effort of will to make herself enter it. The top of the desk was clear, innocent of any papers. She tried one of the drawers, then another. They were locked. Obviously, in spite of what Sandra had said, Mr. Pemberton had not been put out of his stride by the way *she* had treated him. He had been sufficiently self-possessed to put everything neatly away. Where had he put those papers? Could they be in one of these locked drawers or had he put them in her own office? She went back to the smaller room and opened the top drawer of her desk. The papers were laid tidily on the top of her other papers. Another indication that Ronald Pemberton had not been greatly upset by the turn events had taken last night. Perhaps he was used to having his face smacked. She found herself smiling and rejoiced that she was beginning to treat the episode a little more lightly.

She began to type, but with one eye on the clock. Her main concern today was her interview with Mr. Westmacott. He did not usually arrive until ten o'clock. When that time arrived, she must go to his secretary and ask for an appointment. The sooner she had passed this hurdle, the happier she would feel.

'Is it really necessary today? I know that Mr. Westmacott has got an exceptionally busy day today.' Frances Beard stood her ground outside her chief's office as though the main function of her working life was to protect him from ravening wolves. 'Couldn't it wait until tomorrow?'

'No.' Even had it been possible Beverley knew that it would be the same tale tomorrow. It was as difficult to get past Frances Beard as it was to bore through an iron door—or nearly. As she looked at this small, grey-haired woman, Beverley wondered if she would become like her in time. When she had successfully evaded all the attentions of the opposite sex, when they no longer had any interest in her. Miss Beard was a very efficient secretary—Beverley had hoped to be the same. She still bore the traces of early prettiness. As the girl looked at the older woman's primly waved hair, her spotlessly clean, pale blue twin set, the pearls round her neck, her faded pink cheeks, she felt a sudden fear, visualising herself in the years to come. What did she want from the future? She did not want to get married—she would have liked to have children but she did not want the necessary man. Yet again, though, she did not want to turn into another Frances Beard.

'Very well, dear, I will see what I can do. Wait a minute.' Miss Beard vanished into the fastnesses of the head office.

'Mr. Westmacott will see you now.' She was back in a very short time. 'Don't keep him long, will you? He has such a heavy programme today, and he is not as young as he used to be.'

Are any of us? thought the girl as she entered the holy of holies. She knew that the last twelve hours had added much more to her real age than the time warranted.

'Good morning, Beverley,' Mr. Westmacott greeted her. Beverley liked this kindly, elderly gentleman. His blue eyes were always ready to twinkle at the slightest excuse, his lips always ready with a smile. Beverley knew that he could be stern, severe, but only when such an attitude was truly merited. Until today, she had never felt the slightest fear of him. Even today it was not so much fear of him as of herself, as to what she might find herself telling him. She had made up her mind to say a minimum but was aware how hard that might be when she found herself faced with Mr. Westmacott's kindly interest. 'Sit down,' he said now. 'Well, what is this so important business which Miss Beard tells me cannot possibly wait?'

'I want to give in my notice. I want to leave at the end of next week.' She blurted the words out, forgetting all her carefully rehearsed sentences.

'Leave next week!' Mr. Westmacott stared at her in amazement. 'Why, child? Are you not happy here? I had always thought you were so contented.'

'I was. I am. I . . .' She could not go on.

'Is it that you have been offered another post—with better prospects, perhaps? Is that what you are trying to tell me?'

'No. No, I have not got another post to go to, but I want to leave next week.' She kept her eyes down on the desk. She was sure that if she looked at him she would say more than she wanted to. 'I can't tell you my reasons, Mr. Westmacott, but I must leave.' She was ashamed to find her voice rising dangerously high.

'Very well, my dear, if you must, but I shall be very sorry to lose you. We have all valued you very highly.' He looked at her in puzzlement, wondering what lay behind this sudden decision and her evident distress.

'Thank you, Mr. Westmacott. I shall be very sorry to go.' She raised her eyes and scanned his face. Had she sufficient courage to put her next request? 'Do you think I could go into the typing pool for the last week?' She had said it! She sat back, waiting.

'The typing pool! But why? Why...?' He did not ask further. So that was why the girl wanted to leave. Why need Ronald Pemberton drag his love life into the office? He had heard before of the fellow's indulgences in extra-marital affairs, but had decided that it was not his concern since, until now, they had been kept in a separate compartment from his business life. Now they were responsible for the firm losing one of the most promising secretaries they had ever had. How far had it gone? He looked at the girl anxiously.

'You are not in real trouble, are you?' He hesitated to put the question more bluntly. It was not necessary.

'No!'

The ringing indignation reassured him. He did not doubt that she was telling the truth. 'Did you work late last night?' One unpleasant experience would be enough to upset this girl, he decided.

'Y-yes.' Beverley blushed uncomfortably. How many more questions was he going to ask?

'Never mind.' In his desire to know the facts, he had overlooked the fact that his questions could be very embarrassing to a girl of Beverley's nature. 'Of course, you can go into the typing pool if you wish, but I think we had better find some reason for the change. We do not want the other girls to think you have been demoted, do we?'

'No.' That aspect had not struck Beverley before. She had given no thought to the flutter of wagging tongues which her return to the typing pool was likely to set in motion.

'I think I have found a solution.' He had sat for a few moments lost in thought. 'Mr. Pemberton will be wanting a new secretary. If I promote one of the girls from the typing pool she could come to you to learn the ropes. What do you say to that?'

'Thank you, Mr. Westmacott, I think it would be a very good idea.' She felt immensely grateful to this man who, though he had tumbled to the reason for her decision, had said nothing about it openly, had caused her a modicum of embarrassment, and had been sufficiently concerned about her feelings to think up this arrangement. But, she suddenly thought, would it mean her going into Mr. Pemberton's office? 'I should be able to stay in the pool room, shouldn't I?' she asked. 'I should not have to work in the office, should I?'

'No, I think we could arrange that, and I have been thinking I will suggest Mavis Anderson for the position.' A little smile lurked round the corners of his mouth. 'She is quite steady and reliable, and though I don't think Mr. Pemberton will find her ideal, she has got the makings of a competent secretary.' He did not add that Mavis Anderson was also a very plain and unattractive girl, but that smile left very little doubt in Beverley's mind that his choice of Mr. Pemberton's new secretary had not been guided wholly by his knowledge of the girl's capabilities.

Beverley told Sandra that evening of Mr. Westmacott's idea. The arrangement met with her friend's full approval. 'He's a decent old stick, isn't he? It's a pity he's stuck with that old Miss Beard for his secretary. You could just have done with that job.'

'Yes,' agreed Beverley. 'Anyhow, I will have to start looking for something now.'

She scanned the advertisements in the daily papers in vain. Nothing met with her approval. It was in the *Sunday Telegraph* that she finally saw an advertisement which aroused her enthusiasm.

'Listen to this, Sandra,' she exclaimed excitedly. 'Wanted,' she read out, 'competent person—either sex—to catalogue private library. Residential. Write B. Sheavyn, Willerton Grange, Nr. Arnside, Westmorland.'

'What's so special about that? Blast! I can't find the other glove.' She rummaged wildly in a drawer packed with a heterogeneous collection of articles. Both girls were going to church—they attended more or less regularly. Beverley, ready before the other girl, had picked up the paper while she waited. 'Oh, here it is. Read that thing again,' she commanded, prepared to give her attention now.

'But you don't want to go off to Westmorland,' she objected when Beverley had once more read the advertisement. 'And why should that be any better than all the other ones you've turned down? I should think it would be deadly dull.'

'Three reasons.' Beverley had already inwardly listed its merits. 'One—a man who owns a library will probably be fairly old. Two—he probably won't be like these business men, all sex. Three—there won't be other men about. I may be able to work in peace without always being afraid of my boss—or somebody else—getting fresh.'

'O.K., but it's all a case of "might", and I can't see any sense in your leaving London.

Anyhow, we'd better be off now.'

The more Beverley cogitated on the advertisement—and her thoughts were far more occupied with that than with the service—the more it appealed to her.

'I'm going to try for it,' she told Sandra. She had discovered that not a small part of the attraction lay in the idea of living in the country. It meant leaving Sandra of course, but Sandra was so fully occupied with Laurie that her own defection would hardly be the major event it might once have been.

She sent off her application that very afternoon—she had already obtained her testimonial from Mr. Westmacott. She was determined that B. Sheavyn should receive it at the earliest possible moment. She had no idea why she should be so excited about this post, but she was. Was it because it opened a completely fresh vista, a way of life which was as different from anything she had known in the past as a feather bed from a straw mattress? Whatever had made such a comparison come into her head? And which was the feather bed, which the straw mattress? Life up to date had certainly not been a feather bed—there had been far too many pricks and discomforts— like the straw mattress, and existence in a country house might be a cushioned affair. At the moment she felt she would not object to that. Always supposing she got the post, and the advertisement said 'either sex'. That being so, and the world being what it was—a man's world—if a suitable man applied that would be the end of Willerton Grange as far as she was concerned. As she dropped the envelope into the pillar box she sent up a little prayer that no suitable man would apply, that B. Sheavyn would look favourably on her own application.

CHAPTER THREE

'You have got a job on, my boy.' John Sheavyn stood in the centre of the usually spick-and-span library and stared at the disorder which reigned there now. The floor was littered with great wooden crates, a few of them opened with books spilling out, but most of them still in the sealed state in which they had been tossed from the lorry the previous afternoon.

'You're telling me, Grandpa. I had no idea Uncle Jim's library was quite so colossal. Those shelves are not going to be much use.' Bruce Sheavyn looked at the stack of empty shelves which had been prepared to receive this influx. The library was a large room. Its long, graceful windows overlooked the rose garden where a second crop still struggled to make a not-inconsiderable show. The October sun, low now, nearing its nadir, flooded the room with a rosy light. The books opposite took on a rosy tinge. That wall was filled from floor to ceiling with glass-enclosed shelves, all packed with books. 'I shall have to get Rigg in to put up twice as many shelves.'

'It's fortunate we have got a man like Rigg to turn to,' said his grandfather. Thomas Rigg was a craftsman of the old school. He took a pride in his work, in the dove-tailing which was an essential part of every piece of work he did. He was now nearing seventy but was always willing to do any task which John Sheavyn might ask of him. He, his father and his grandfather before him had worked for John Sheavyn and his forbears for more years than either could number.

'It's not going to end with Tom's work. Those books are going to need cataloguing. Uncle Jim can't have had any system. From the cases we have already opened it is obvious that they have all been thrown in anyhow and there is no list with them. It will take a knowledgeable person months, maybe years for all I know, to get them in order and catalogued. It strikes me Uncle Jim's legacy, as far as this part is concerned, is a bit of a white elephant.'

'You'll be proud of it some day, Bruce. A library such as this will be is an acquisition to any house. I have always felt ours was inadequate. Neither your father nor I ever added to it. Unless I am very much mistaken you will find that Jim's library is a mine of modern as well as old works.'

'Yes, Grandpa, I'm sure you are right. In fact, I know you are. Uncle Jim had books of every type under the sun, but I didn't realise in the days when I used to visit him that his

40

library was quite so unwieldy. Anyhow, I mustn't forget that Uncle Jim's legacy included a hefty sum of money—more than enough to pay somebody to get his library into order. I think I had better set about advertising as soon as possible.'

'Yes, I should. There will be plenty of young women who would find such a job congenial. It would have to be resident, wouldn't it?'

'Yes.' Bruce Sheavyn stood lost in thought. 'But I would rather have a man,' he said finally.

'A man! Why? You will find it very hard to get the right sort of young man to take a post like that. It does not lead anywhere.'

'I know that, Grandpa. Nevertheless, I can't have a woman.' He was obviously distressed, but equally obviously, obdurate. 'You know perfectly well, sir,' he broke out desperately as his grandfather still showed no signs of being convinced, 'that Cora would never get on with another woman in the house.' Even the maids were continually changing—there had been a constant succession in the six years of their marriage; it would be still worse with a woman of equal status. No such woman would be likely to tolerate her fits of unreasoning temper, added to which there might be the complication of jealousy on Cora's part. He would have said that she did not care enough about him for that, but one never knew.

'Aye, I'd not thought of that.' He tried to hide his look of commiseration. This grandson of his, so satisfactory in every other way, had made—in his grandfather's eyes—a disastrous marriage. He could not restrain the words which came to his lips. 'I can't understand the woman. I ... Sorry, lad,' he finished as his grandson gave him an angry look. Privately he thought he had been most moderate. He could have said so much more. 'So you are going to advertise for a young man?'

'Advertise for a young man. Why are you going to advertise for a young man, Bruce?' The door had opened unperceived by either of them. 'What's it all about?' This was one of the occasions when Cora Sheavyn chose to put up a façade of affection for her husband, a façade which infuriated the old man. The fact that she had completely ignored his presence had nothing to do with his annoyance. He had long been aware that his lack of appreciation of his grandson's wife was more than reciprocated. He had often thought that if she had not been afraid of the consequences, Cora Sheavyn would already have found some means of furnishing him with a fatal dose.

'Grandpa and I were just saying that we

should need somebody to catalogue this lot,' he gestured to the surrounding medley, 'to make some order out of this chaos.'

'Sell the lot, is what I should say, but I don't for a minute suppose that you will take my advice. Anyhow, come along now. We can discuss it over our drinks. If you don't come now there will be no time for them before dinner. I had been wondering what you were up to.' She eased him gradually towards the door.

'Will you join us, Grandpa?' Bruce made the suggestion, though he had very little hope that his grandfather would accept his offer. His wife's treatment of the old man, his grandfather's scarcely concealed dislike of Cora, were but two of the troubles which his marriage had brought in its train. He had tried hard to shut his eyes to these other troubles— it was impossible to blind himself to the knowledge of their aversion to each other— but he had to admit to himself latterly that he had made the mistake of a lifetime when he had allowed himself to be married by Cora Marrow—he knew now that it was she who had initiated the courtship, she who had brought it to its consummation.

'Pah!' John Sheavyn watched their retreating backs, shut the door loudly behind them. 'If the lad had only seen her back view

43

one could have understood it,' he said. Seen from the rear, Cora Sheavyn could easily have passed for a girl of twenty. Her slim figure, sheathed in a perfectly fitting, fine wool, green dress was crowned by a head of immaculately dressed tawny hair. John Sheavyn scornfully told himself that any woman who visited an expensive hairdresser twice a week could look as well groomed. The shortness of the green dress revealed a pair of shapely legs encased in the sheerest of stockings, stockings long enough to make sure that even the near-mini length of the dress could never cause its wearer the slightest embarrassment.

'Mutton, dressed up as lamb.' It was by phrases such as this that he tried to work off his irritation. He knew that many of them were unfair. He did not know how many years older than her husband Cora was, but she admitted to four. He did not think he would be making an overstatement if he put the difference at ten years. That would make the woman forty, at least. Bruce had only been twenty-four when he had married. Forty could not exactly qualify for the label 'mutton' but it was too old in his opinion—biased, he admitted—to sport skirts of that length—or shortness!

'I suppose I'm old-fashioned,' he muttered, 'but I don't suppose I should be half as critical if I did not dislike the woman so much.' He turned from the door and began to toy with the books, placing them haphazardly on the empty shelves, seeking by the employment of his hands to curb the trend of his thoughts. 'Yes, Matthew?' The door had opened and an elderly man came in with a tray.

'Your sherry, sir. Dinner will be ready in a quarter of an hour.'

'Thank you, Matthew. Put it there, will you?' He indicated a small table near the window. Pulling a chair close to it he sat down, willing the mellowness of the wine and the scene beyond the window to imbue him with their own mellowness, to imbue him with a greater sense of charitableness, less irritation before he joined his grandson—and wife—for dinner.

Willerton Grange was more than large enough to allow the two households to live separately—completely so, had they so desired. Bruce Sheavyn had never had any other thought than that he should return to his old home when they married—the home to which he had become heir when his father was killed over Germany. He had only been two years old then. Nor had he any thought that his grandfather would abdicate when he brought his wife home. Cora had hinted— more than hinted—that his grandfather ought to move to a smaller house and leave his grandson in possession of the Grange. Bruce had replied that the Grange belonged to the old man and that, even if that were not the case, the house was sufficiently commodious to house them all happily. Even had he not been very attached to the grandfather who had acted as both father and mother to him—his mother had fallen a victim to a flying bomb soon after her husband's death—he would never have suggested that the old man should leave the home which had been his from birth, to which he was wedded by all the traditions of generations of Sheavyns having lived at Willerton Grange.

'Have you decided how you are going to set about getting this young man for the library? Where will you advertise?' They were all three seated at the dinner table now. Dinner was the one meal when the two households formally converged. Bruce and his wife had the left wing for their exclusive use, with their own domestic staff, but it had been agreed when the arrangement was first made that the young people should dine with John Sheavyn in the main dining-room except on such occasions as when they wished to entertain their own friends. John had often wished that he had never initiated such an arrangement. There were times when the meal was sheer purgatory, when the effort to keep a rein on his tongue came near to bursting a blood vessel. It was Cora who answered him now.

'I have told Bruce that it is throwing money away to spend all that money on a librarian. Who will ever want to read all those old books, or any of them, come to that? I expect if it was offered for sale as a whole library it would fetch quite a price. There always seem to be some fools in the world to buy that sort of thing.'

Neither man made a reply. They were both aware that her intention was merely to annoy. She knew quite well that her husband would not contemplate selling his uncle's legacy and that his grandfather would be of the same mind. Bruce turned to his grandfather.

'I have been thinking about it and I think the Personal column of the *Sunday Telegraph* might fill the bill, better than the ordinary appointments page. What do you think?'

'And get some pansy. That's the only sort of man who would answer such an advertisement.' Cora once more intervened.

'Then...' John Sheavyn stopped himself just in time. He had almost said that they would get someone like her brother. And he was being unfair again. Why did that woman always bring out the worst in him? Gilbert Marrow was a good-looking weakling,

47

nothing worse, nor had he ever really thought so. 'This is just the place for him to blush unseen,' he finished lamely. 'Or is it the violet which does that?' He went on hurriedly. 'That reminds me, did I ever tell you that tale about . . .' He dug out an apt tale from his vast repertoire. Damn it, why did Cora invariably make him feel so uncomfortable?

He finished his tale. Bruce laughed heartily—he had always been appreciative of his grandfather's gift for the apt tale. One glance at the woman's face told him that it had been received by her with the usual poker face. He turned away quickly, trying to hide the expression of distaste which he knew was only too obvious. Where were Bruce's senses when he married that woman? One look at her fact ought to have told any man what her nature was. She was perfectly made up, but no make-up could hide the sharpness of the features, the drooping lips. Art had done something to disguise the thinness of those but it could not hide the droop. She had the fox-like, or should he say vixen, looks which were sometimes an accompaniment to that tawny hair.

'How's the leg today, Bruce?' he asked. It might seem to be a complete change of subject, but it followed on logically from his thoughts. Had his grandson not had the accident which had left him not only with a slight limp, but also with intermittent pain, he would never have met, never have married this woman. If only it had been a hundred miles away from Cora Marrow's home instead of a mere five miles, how different might life have been now, not only for Bruce but also for his grandfather.

As the old man looked at his grandson across the well-appointed table—its gleaming silver and glistening glass bearing witness to the loving care lavished upon it by Matthew and his wife—he wondered why Bruce should have had to pay so heavily for that one youthful error. That reckless driving—he had been doing over eighty on a country road when he had come into collision with another car— had not only left him with a perpetual limp, but had saddled him with a wife who, his grandfather was convinced, would become more and more of a trial as the years went on.

The owner of that other car had been Gilbert Marrow. Gilbert had come off with very minor injuries, they had not even necessitated his being kept in hospital. He had, however, visited Bruce a number of times while the latter was there and when he learned that Bruce would have to have several operations on his leg, spaced over a number of weeks, had suggested that the young man should spend the intervening weeks at his, Gilbert's, home, which he shared with his sister.

Cora Marrow, thirty-five years old and unmarried, had made the most of her opportunities. As a young woman she had the power to attract the opposite sex, but her sharp tongue and easily roused temper had rendered those attractions short-lived. Worse still, as far as she was concerned, the local grapevine let it be known that Cora Marrow's surface charm camouflaged a nature which was the reverse of charming. It was years now since she had had the chance to exercise those charms, but she had learned her lesson. She had managed to acquire a certain amount of wisdom and self-control and the Cora Marrow who played hostess to Bruce Sheavyn during those weeks of waiting was, or seemed to be, a woman of charm and sympathy. It was not surprising that her guest succumbed to her wiles. It was not until her claws were truly and thoroughly embedded that Bruce Sheavyn had any idea of the claws buried beneath the velvet, and it was still longer before he realised how sharp they were and, also, how easily they were unsheathed, how allied they were to the feline spitting and snarling which he discovered to be yet another characteristic of the woman he had married.

50

She can't even give him a child, thought John Sheavyn. It was six years since they had married and there had never been a whisper of one, and the woman was getting older and older every day. It would not be so very long before she was too old for child-bearing—if she wanted it—and every indication at present was that she had no such desire. The chances of an heir to Willerton Grange were very slim. That question, 'How's the leg?' was only too natural a sequence to thoughts of Cora.

'Quite good today, Grandpa.' When did the lad ever make any other reply? And what a youngster he still looked. It was the fair skin, the bright hair with the unruly quiff, the lithe figure which gave him that boyish appearance, and the proximity of that woman only heightened the effect of youth. She looked old enough to be his mother. No, she did not. There he went again, being thoroughly unfair to the woman. Thanks to the time and money spent on her appearance she barely looked her age. Nevertheless, she did look years older than her husband. 'Are you going to be busy tonight, Grandpa?' He retrieved his wandering thoughts ready to answer the question but Bruce went on. 'Something cropped up at the works today that I should like to consult you about.' Bruce was in charge of the family works at Kendal. John Sheavyn occasionally put in an appearance, but since his grandson's return to health those appearances had become comparatively rare.

'No, I'm doing nothing special. Come whenever you are ready.'

'I do think that you might remember that you have got a wife who has been alone all day.' Cora's mouth turned down even more than usual.

'I'm sorry, Cora, but it's important, and you know that if I do stay with you you will only be watching television.' Cora was a non-stop television addict, a non-selective watcher. Her husband had learned to read through it to a certain extent—Cora insisted on her need for her husband's company in spite of the fact that the busy screen, the blaring accompaniment, precluded the possibility of companionship other than the mere physical presence. Bruce felt that since he could give her so little in the way of real love—though he doubted whether she had any conception of the state of his feelings—it was incumbent on him, as far as possible, to give her what she asked. Nevertheless, there were times when he felt that one more silly joke, piercing insistently his efforts to read, would make him put his fist through the pictured face which mouthed those jokes. Then he sought refuge with his grandfather. Tonight he had a legitimate excuse. There was no need to wait for the inane sally, the answering raucous laughter to drive him forth.

'This is good.' He stretched at ease in the chair before his grandfather's roaring fire. The old man's sanctum was an all-male room. The deep, leather armchairs had been there ever since Bruce could remember. There was none of the prettiness which characterised the room in which Cora was watching television, none of the feminine touches which Bruce found so irritating. He had grown up in an all-male household and Cora was not the woman to reconcile him to anything else. He had to tolerate the atmosphere in the left wing, but toleration was as far as he could go. He pulled out his pipe. He was not really a smoker. Cora was a compulsive one, smoking one cigarette after another, but Bruce usually limited himself to the one pipe which he smoked in his grandfather's company. Tonight he started right away on the subject which had prompted his visit.

'That man Wilcox is a trouble-maker, sir. If we don't watch out, there will be a real flare-up before long.' He went on to tell what had happened that day, to discuss the advisability of giving the obstreperous Wilcox his cards.

'I will go down myself tomorrow,' said the older man. 'I'll have a straight talk with him and let him know that this is his last chance. And I think we had better call a meeting of the lot of them in the dinner hour. We never have had trouble at Sheavyn's works and I do not intend to have it now.'

Bruce looked with admiration at this little man. At seventy-nine he was as clear-sighted, as forceful as many a man twenty years younger. 'That ugly little old man.' That was what Cora had called him. He was a little man and he could certainly never have been handsome. He looked, perhaps, like a wise old monkey, a kindly monkey. His face was scored with the lines of humour. 'That reminds me of a tale' might have been his grandfather's signature tune. He not only had an admirable memory, but it was always on tap. There were few occasions when he could not supply the apt tale, and to the memory was added the gift of getting it over. There was no scamping of telling detail when his grandfather told a tale, no hurrying over the denouement. He was a born raconteur. The last year or so the occasions which had brought forth his quips and anecdotes had become rarer. Bruce realised that this was due in part to the fact that he went to business less often, made fewer contacts, had little opportunity of adding new grist to his mill, but he also knew that Cora's scornful reception of the old man's jokes had done much towards drying them up at source.

It was several days later that he showed his grandfather the replies to his advertisement. He had finally decided to envisage the possibility of a woman, and as it turned out there were only women applicants.

'They seem a poor lot on the whole,' he said. 'The only one I fancy at all is this Beverley Gordon, and she's very young. Still, I have to go up to London soon to see that agent, so I'll see her then. If she's no use I will advertise again.' He repressed a sigh as he turned away. It was no use telling his grandfather that it was Cora's reaction that bothered him. How would she respond to the idea of having a young woman of twenty as an intimate member of the family? He could see squalls ahead.

CHAPTER FOUR

It was less than a fortnight after this that Beverley Gordon found herself in a northward bound train, on her way to take up the position of librarian at Willerton Grange. Her exit from London proved not only to be an unheralded affair—Sandra was working that Saturday morning and was unable to see her off—it also turned out to be an undignified scramble.

'Don't leave old Horsey time for a sob-making farewell,' Sandra had warned her. Miss Horsfall was notorious for the amount of pathos she could put into these leave-takings.

Mindful of this warning, Beverley had allowed herself the minimum of time to reach the station. It was not until she was in the warden's office that she discovered that her watch was slow.

'Goodbye, Miss...' As she held out her hand she caught sight of the electric wall clock. 'That clock's not right, is it?' she gasped.

'Yes, I think so.' Miss Horsfall glanced at her wrist. 'Yes, it's right.'

'Gosh! I must fly.' She was out of the room in a flash, having bid the briefest of goodbyes. The warden stared after her. The modern generation of young people just had no manners, she told herself, but she had expected better of Beverley Gordon. She was the last girl from whom she would have expected such a cursory farewell. She could not have stage-managed a more hurried departure.

But Beverley had not stage-managed her farewell to such an extent. She was almost frantic with anxiety when she left the warden's room. What would she do if she missed that train? She was being met at Arnside. She breathed a sigh of relief as a taxi came cruising along. She hailed it and within a few minutes was at Euston station. She rushed to the departure platform—fortunately she had booked her ticket previously—and reached it just as the guard was about to raise his green flag. A porter seized her case and pushed her into the first available carriage. The whistle blew, the train started. She was really on her way to Willerton Grange.

She put her suitcase on the rack, looked round and found that there was still one corner seat unoccupied. After a brief survey of her fellow passengers—a family of father, mother and two children at the other end of the compartment, an elderly woman immediately opposite her—she lost herself in her own thoughts. Inevitably they flew back to the previous Tuesday, to her interview with Bruce Sheavyn.

She had worn the red coat and the fur hat in which Sandra had pronounced that she looked 'smashing', but in spite of the fact that she knew she was looking her best she had felt more nervous than at any previous interview. 'As though it matters all that much,' she had chided herself. 'It isn't the only job under the sun.' But she had begun to think that it was, that if she did not get this post she would never find another which was so just what she wanted.

It was still only ten minutes to twelve when she reached the restaurant where Bruce Sheavyn had arranged to meet her. Ten more minutes to waste, but she felt she could not dawdle in Oxford Street any longer. She went up the stairs and sat down in the little vestibule adjoining the main room. At this hour there was very little traffic through it. Two or three customers went through to the restaurant, one or two stood having drinks at the bar. None showed any interest in Beverley. When the swing doors opened to admit a young man in his twenties Beverley merely thought it was just another customer, but after one glance at the girl he came straight across to her.

'Miss Gordon?' he asked.

'Yes.' She was too taken aback to get out

58

more than the brief syllable. She had derided Sandra's suggestion that her possible employer might be a young man. Sandra had agreed and had even referred to him later as Beverley's 'old codger'. Her lips twisted as she thought of this.

'I'm Bruce Sheavyn,' he said. 'What's the joke?' Her amusement had not gone unnoticed.

'I had a shock.' Beverley smiled naturally this time. 'I was expecting someone much older. You are so different from my picture of you.'

'Sorry.' Bruce Sheavyn laughed. 'I suppose you thought anybody who could have a library of such proportions as to need a librarian to catalogue it would be well on the way to his grave.'

'More or less,' she agreed.

'It is a legacy from my uncle and though I am very pleased to have it, it really is rather a headache. But shall we discuss that over lunch?' He led the way into the restaurant. Beverley noticed that he limped. Why? she wondered. He was far too young for it to be a war injury. 'I chose this place because it is so quiet. It never is very crowded and the tables are wide apart. It is one of the few places in London where you can hear yourself speak in the lunch hour.'

They found a table for two, and while Bruce Sheavyn ordered, having first ascertained his companion's wishes, Beverley studied her hoped-for future employer. He is nice, I like him, she decided. As the meal progressed she became still more confirmed in her first appraisal. This, she felt sure, was a man she would like to work for, there was nothing of the sleek business man about him. He was as different as possible from Mr. Pemberton.

'Your testimonial says that you were in charge of your school library.'

'Yes.' She went on to explain what this had entailed. Trying to sell myself, she thought, but if she had been anxious to obtain this post before she set eyes on Bruce Sheavyn she was doubly so now. She felt, even as she told herself that such a feeling was utterly foolish, that she could not bear the thought of this young man going out of her life for ever.

Bruce Sheavyn was trying to conduct this interview in a businesslike manner, but he could not help wondering what Cora would say if he appointed such an attractive girl. Mentally he shrugged. The girl had got all the qualifications, seemed a thoroughly nice girl. Cora would be certain to disapprove of any woman whom he might appoint and she most assuredly would quarrel with an older one.

'Could you start on Saturday?' he said

finally. 'I mean come up on Saturday and start work on Monday.'

'Yes.' Once again Beverley found the word all that she could manage. Her heart was beating uncomfortably fast. Now that this interview was brought to a successful conclusion she was tongue-tied. With an effort she pulled herself together. 'I shall be very pleased to come.' The words came out with a rush.

She had been almost beside herself with elation when she had left Bruce Sheavyn. Sitting in the train which was now taking her to his home, she found herself giggling at the recollection. She had walked along Oxford Street in a dream, but an irate matron had speedily dragged her back to earth.

'Can't you look where you are going?' she had demanded angrily, clutching frantically at a dog lead, at the other end of which a white poodle was busily engaged in wrapping the intervening part round Beverley's legs.

'I'm sorry.' She had perforce come to a halt. 'Give me the lead, will you?' There was no means of disengaging herself from the poodle's chain than by unanchoring it from its mistress. 'That's all right now.' She handed the lead back to the poodle's owner, receiving no thanks, only a second intimidating glare. As she turned to look at the woman's receding bulk she decided that this was not the first time, and it probably would not be the last, that the poodle had suffered a similar involvement.

'It's mad taking a poodle shopping in Oxford Street,' she had said, but she had also realised that it was equally foolish to treat the paving stones of that thoroughfare as though they were the Elysian fields. The encounter with the lady and her poodle might not have been wholly her fault, but unless she mended her ways the next *contretemps* might not only be her own culpability but have more serious consequences. Oxford Street was no more the place for a dream walker than it was for a poodle attached at one end of a chain to a mountain of flesh.

There was no such bar to dreaming now, and dream she did, until finally even dreaming palled. At last the long journey drew to its close. Beverley had acquainted herself beforehand with the train's route, with the times of its arrival at the different stations. When they reached Carnforth she began to throw off the lethargy which had seeped through her as the train hummocked on and on. Only one more station, Silverdale, before she reached her destination.

'Arnside!' She opened the carriage door and stepped on to the platform. She had no time to take stock of her surroundings before she was greeted by an elderly man in a chauffeur's uniform.

'Miss Gordon?'

'Yes.' Beverley felt her spirits fall. She had expected that Bruce Sheavyn would have met her.

'Mr. Bruce asked me to meet you as he had to wait in for an important telephone call.' He took Beverley's case and led the way to an impressive-looking car. 'Would you care to travel in the front, miss?'

'Yes, please.' Beverley's first reaction had been to opt for the anonymity of the back seat, but she remembered Sandra's advice of the previous evening. 'For goodness' sake,' she had said. 'Do make an effort to come out of your shell in this new job.'

The short drive proved Sandra right in this case. It was no ordeal at all, rather the reverse. Matthew—everybody calls me Matthew, the old man had said—pointed out the places of interest as they drove along the quiet country roads. 'That's Arnside Tower.' He pointed to a grey ruin standing on a rising piece of ground. 'And that's the Knott. It used to be a real pretty place afore they did all this building, bungalows and what-have-you. I can't see why folks need to come and spoil our countryside,' he grumbled.

63

'Have you lived here long, Matthew?' she asked.

'All my life, and that's over sixty years. And my father before me, and his father before that.'

It was hardly surprising, thought Beverley, that the old man felt sore about the rash of building which was changing the face of the country. She encouraged him to talk of the district as it had been when he was a boy, a subject on which he was more than ready to discourse. It seemed no time before they turned off the road through an old stone gateway and along a tree-fringed drive which opened out in the midst of a garden before an imposing stone mansion. Matthew got out and rang the bell before he opened the car door for Beverley.

'Guess the missus'll be in the kitchen,' he explained. 'She was baking when I came out.' The wait that followed his words pointed to the probability that Matthew's wife had her arms elbow-deep in pastry, but the door did open at last to reveal a buxom, rosy-cheeked woman, several years younger than her husband.

'Sorry I was so long, but I'm in the middle of baking,' she apologised. 'I...' her husband cut her short.

'This is Miss Gordon, Florence. Will you

64

take her straight in to Mr. Bruce? He's in the library. I'll take her bag upstairs and then put the car away.'

'Come away in.' Florence ushered Beverley into a large panelled hall and was about to knock on a door when a woman came running into the hall from a passage at the far end.

'Yer cakes is burnin', Mrs. Benson,' she cried.

Florence Benson turned at once.

'Excuse me, miss, I must go. You just knock on that door and Mr. Bruce'll call you.' She followed the woman with a speed which Beverley would have imagined to be impossible for a woman of her bulk.

'I'll kill him myself if you don't get a move on.' A woman's shrill voice halted her hand as she raised it to knock.

'I tell you I will do it, but in my own time.' Beverley recognised this voice. It belonged to Bruce Sheavyn. She stood aghast. Who were they going to kill? She shook herself angrily. It could not be anything like that, but she had not time to think about that now. She had got to go into that room, the room from which those ominous sentences had come, but she could not let them know that she had overheard those words—whatever they meant. Her hand dropped from the door, she paced slowly up and down the hall, praying

65

that the door would not open before she again summoned the courage to knock, or that Florence Benson would not emerge from her nether regions and demand a reason for her continued presence in the hall.

'Come in.' At last the moment had come when she deemed it politic to knock. Bruce Sheavyn's voice summoned her to enter. She had no eyes for the lovely room, pleasing in spite of its disorder. Her eyes were all for the man and woman standing there—Bruce Sheavyn coming to meet her, the woman standing by the window, her back to the room. And what a back! thought Beverley; that glorious hair, the marvellous figure, and the perfectly fitting, light blue jersey suit. It must have cost the earth. Bruce Sheavyn had certainly got a beautiful wife. She must be his wife. So he had got a wife. She had guessed as much when she heard those two voices beyond the closed door, but it was only now that the fact really registered. She could not hide from herself that the news was unwelcome. What had she been hoping for? Surely there had been no truth in Sandra's teasing remarks.

'Good afternoon, Miss Gordon. I hope you had a good journey. Do come and sit by the fire. Cora,' he addressed the figure in the window. 'This is Miss Gordon. Do you think we might ring for tea now,' he added as the woman turned.

'Oh, no!' Beverley just stopped herself from saying the words aloud. They were not a negation of a desire for tea, they were the result of shock, shock caused when Mrs. Sheavyn turned round. The front view was so very different from the back, at least the part that mattered. The hair, from the front, was even more beautiful than from behind, but the face it framed was far from beautiful. It was years older than she had pictured, but that was only part of the disillusionment. The sharp features were creased in lines of ill-temper, the eyes were narrowed in anger. The artificial smile which she summoned up as she turned was a travesty of a smile, it only served to heighten the original impression of a temper which had an evil quality.

'How do you do, Miss Gordon?' There was a saccharine sweetness in the tone which matched the smile but was wholly at war with the basic expression. 'I am sure you must be dying for a cup of tea after that long journey.' She had got herself in hand now. The smile had attained a near genuine quality, but Beverley found that she still did not like it.

It was a relief when Florence appeared with the tea tray. Husband and wife each addressed their remarks to Beverley; the interchange of hostilities was too recent, had been too sharp, to admit of an immediate truce. Even the business of tea-drinking did not loosen Cora's tongue as far as her husband was concerned. She received his civilities with a tight-lipped silence which served to emphasise the over-gushing note in the remarks which she addressed to the newcomer. Beverley sensed the relief with which Bruce eventually rose from his chair—it found an echo in her own feelings.

'Would you like to see your own rooms now, Miss Gordon?' he asked. 'I will show you the layout of the house as we go.' He stood by the door for a moment. 'This, of course, will be your work-room. I must say I don't envy you your job at this stage. If it were me I should not know where to start.'

'No, it will be a bit of a problem.' Beverley looked with a momentary dismay at the scattered books, the cases pushed to one end of the room. 'I expect I shall soon work out a system,' she said more hopefully than she felt.

'Matthew will open those cases for you when you are ready, but my grandfather and I thought that they would probably be best left as they are until you have made some order out of the present chaos.'

'Yes.' So the family was not restricted to Bruce Sheavyn and his wife. There was also a grandfather. Were there any other members of the family living here? Beverley wondered. The place certainly looked large enough to house any number of relations. She followed Bruce into the hall. He led the way to the far end—the hall stretched the whole length of this part of the building, it was indeed a large room with windows at the end opposite the front door. Bruce Sheavyn went to the windows and looked out.

'The house is built round three sides of a rectangle, as you can see,' he said. 'This part houses the library and the dining-room,' he pointed to the further of two doors on the wall facing the library, 'and above is the drawing-room, the master bedroom, which is never used now, and the gallery. I will take you to see that later. The left wing of the house is now our domain, my wife's and mine, and the right wing is the bedrooms and kitchen quarters. That is where your suite is and my grandfather has his next to yours.'

Suite! Beverley wondered if her ears had deceived her. Surely she would not be provided with a suite. It sounded a very far cry from half a bed-sitting-room. She stood by the man's side looking at the scene beyond the window. The three sides of the rectangle were walls of the same mellowed stone as the front of the house; stone walls pleasantly spaced with stone-framed windows. A lawn, bearing witness to years of loving care, almost filled the rectangle—there was a rose-bed in the centre, paths ran round the three sides. The fourth side spread out into a large garden, bounded on the farthest side by a wood, the trees of which shone golden brown in the rays of the setting sun.

'How lovely!' she exclaimed.

'Yes, it is, isn't it? I love this old place, everything about it.' He moved from the window and led the way along a wide corridor—a corridor which stretched in both directions from the hall, the whole length of the main building. One side was bounded by windows overlooking the quadrangle, the other was panelled in the same wood as the hall.

'There are the kitchen quarters,' he pointed along another passage which turned off at right angles to the main corridor, not quite so wide but equally bright, equally well windowed. 'We go up here to your rooms.' He halted at the top of the graceful staircase. 'That is my grandfather's suite,' he indicated one door, 'and this yours,' opening another. 'I hope you will find it comfortable. I am afraid it is rather old-fashioned, but so is the whole house except for our wing and the kitchens. Grandfather had those modernised, but he says he is happier with things as they are.

Time enough to modernise when I come into it, he says, but I have a strong suspicion that if I please myself I shall not do overmuch in the way of modernisation.' A tiny sigh escaped but he choked it back. Beverley, remembering the scene which she had interrupted, guessed that his wife might prove a stumbling block, that she might not be content with things as they were.

They were now in a small vestibule with three doors opening off it. Bruce Sheavyn threw one of them open.

'Your sitting-room,' he announced. 'The bedroom,' as he opened the second, 'and the bathroom.'

Beverley stood tongue-tied. Even had the rooms been small and poorly furnished she would have thought herself lucky to be the sole owner of three rooms, but the sitting-room and the bedroom were both gracious rooms, with tall graceful windows. Both were furnished comfortably and tastefully, even if the taste was that of a generation of which Beverley knew little except from hearsay. The bathroom she found quite awe-inspiring. It was nearly as large as the bed-sitting-room she had shared for the last two years. The big bath was encased in mahogany, a wood which was in evidence in all the other fittings.

'I hope you won't mind it being so

antiquated,' Bruce asked, uncertain as to whether the young woman's silence was due to dismay. He realised that it was quite possible that to a modern young lady, the décor might appear ludicrous. For him, who had grown up with it, there was definitely an attraction in it, but he was ready to admit that he was sentimentally biased, and that it would not be to everyone's taste.

'Oh, no, I love it,' cried Beverley. 'I think it most attractive and it looks awfully comfortable.'

In fact comfort was definitely the operative word. Two deep velvet-covered armchairs flanked the fireplace in which a fire burned brightly. A thick, multi-patterned carpet covered the floor; the small table, the bookcase, the desk, were all in mahogany, polished to a mirror-like sheen. Beverley thought she had never seen so much mahogany grouped so closely in the whole of her life. Her mother's home had been furnished completely in oak—cheaper and easier to keep decent, her mother had said. The only modern touch in all these rooms was the white, flower-embroidered candlewick bedspread, and even that, if Beverley had realised it, was a modern harkback to an old fashion.

'Well, I will leave you to settle in now. If

you want anything ring that bell and either Matthew or Florence will come. Dinner will be at seven. We all have it together in the dining-room. You will be able to find your way there, won't you?'

'Oh, yes, thank you.'

'Good. I will see you then.' He raised a hand in a gesture of farewell and was gone. Beverley flopped into one of the easy chairs.

'Gosh, it's fabulous,' she muttered, stretching out her hands towards the blazing coals. 'It's just out of this world.' She thought of the suitcase in the next room waiting to be unpacked. 'It can wait,' she said. 'There's plenty of time. I'm just going to enjoy myself now.' She lay back in the chair and allowed herself to dream and think.

It is like a fairy tale, she thought. Poor little working girl goes to live in country mansion. But there is no prince, she remembered. Bruce Sheavyn could not be cast for that part; he was married. Otherwise he would have fitted the part very well. Perhaps there was a brother. No brother had been mentioned but that did not mean anything. There had been no mention of a wife or a grandfather when she had been interviewed. She felt that she could hardly wait until seven o'clock to find out whether there were any more members of this family. The thought of dinner brought her up sharp. What ought she to wear? She had bought several new dresses during those last few days in London, but was at a loss to know which was the most suitable. She finally decided on a simple, well-cut, long-sleeved dress of a deep blue.

'I don't look too bad,' she said as she looked in the mirror, 'but I shall have to let my hair grow. It's far too short.' She went down to the dining-room with what was, for her, a certain amount of assurance.

'This is Miss Gordon, Grandpa.' Beverley's hand was grasped firmly by a little old man who reminded her of a character in *Snow-white*—except that he had not got a beard, only a small moustache.

He is sweet, she thought, as she looked at the kind face, deeply scored by laughter lines. Her first impression was intensified as she found herself responding to his kindly interest, though she early realised that his daughter-in-law regarded him very differently. Though she certainly seemed to be in a more amiable frame of mind than she had been at the girl's first sight of her—she was quite pleasant to her husband and consistently attentive to Beverley—she hardly deigned a word to the old gentleman. If she had to address him it was as Mr. Sheavyn. It was obvious that she repudiated the thought of any relationship between them.

'You are going to find it very quiet here, Miss Gordon, aren't you?' John Sheavyn asked the question quite early in the meal, just as Beverley put down her soup spoon on her empty plate.

'I don't think so, sir. I think I shall like it. I am looking forward to the quietness after the bustle of London.'

'Have you always lived in London?' John Sheavyn was asking all the questions which his grandson had not asked at the interview.

'No, only since my mother died, though we lived quite close before that.'

'No father?'

'No.' Beverley hesitated. Part of her felt that she should resent this probing into her private life, but the old man's interest was so obviously kindly. There was no question of prying. 'My father left my mother when I was seven years old.'

'H-hm. That was hard on you.' The old man went on with his catechism. 'Any brothers or sisters?' he asked.

'No, I was an only child.'

'Like Bruce here,' commented John Sheavyn. 'I always think that this only child business is a mistake. In my youth people went in for large families. Much better all round.'

'Implying that I am thoroughly spoilt, Grandpa?'

'You're not so bad.' The grandfather could not keep the pride out of his voice nor yet from his eyes. 'Considering everything you have not turned out so badly.' It was patent that he considered his words the height of understatement, that his grandson was his joy and pride.

And well he might be, thought Beverley. Then she remembered the words she had overheard. There must be some explanation for them. They could not mean what they sounded like. Whatever his wife might do, and Beverley felt that she would not like to have to answer for Cora Sheavyn, Bruce would never contemplate the action which the words implied. Cora had said 'I'll kill him myself.' Him! But 'him' might apply to an animal, she thought suddenly. This was the country where animals abounded. It would be some pet, a cat or a dog, which was old or ill, or it might even be a horse. She breathed an almost audible sigh of relief at this solution, and then realised that John Sheavyn was addressing her.

'And how will you occupy yourself? Are you a reader?'

'Yes, I am very fond of reading.' She was beginning to feel restive under the stream of questions. She liked the old man, but he did seem to want to know a lot about her.

'You realise you are welcome to borrow any of the books in the library, don't you?' It was Bruce Sheavyn speaking this time. 'I don't know what sort of things you like but I should think my uncle's library should cater for most tastes—from modern novels to the ancients, poetry, travel, what have you.'

'I suppose it is too much to hope that you play chess.' John Sheavyn spoke wistfully. Since Bruce's marriage his opportunities for a game of chess had been very curtailed. Though the young man did sometimes manage to put in a game with his grandfather, these occasions were looked upon with scant favour by his wife, and as the years had gone on his few chess cronies had either died or become too old or enfeebled to make the effort.

'But I do.' Beverley had been a member of the chess club at school and had held her own bravely with the boys who formed the main body of the club.

'Good!' The old man's face was wreathed in smiles. 'We will have a match soon. I won't ask you tonight, but we might manage tomorrow perhaps.'

'Well, it doesn't look as though you will do too badly for inside entertainment.' There was a suspicion of a sneer behind the words. Beverley suspected rightly that Cora Sheavyn resented the friendliness of the other two. She had not known what to think when Bruce had announced that he had engaged a young woman. 'Young and immature,' he had said, 'but she seems as though she knows her job.' She had resolved to wait and see what the girl was like before she decided on her reaction. She was still waiting.

For the rest of the meal-time conversation was more general. The old man seemed to have exhausted his questions for the time being. When they had finished they all went their separate ways.

'Matthew will bring your breakfast to your room,' Bruce told Beverley. 'Do what you like during the morning. We meet here for mid-day dinner at one.'

Good nights were said and Beverley went upstairs to her own apartments. She felt excited, elated. Her first meal had gone off satisfactorily. She felt as content and well fed as a cat who has just had a saucer of cream. The meal had undoubtedly done its share to enduing her with this feeling of well-being. Now I know what gracious living is like, she thought. There had been nothing ostentatious about either the food or its manner of serving, but the contrast with the hostel meals was unbelievable, even the difference from meals at home when her mother was alive. Beverley's visits to Sandra's home had made her realise how different were the meals of a household composed of two women from those of a family, but the meals at Sandra's bore no resemblance to the meal which she had just sat through. There, everything, everybody was happy-go-lucky. It was the difference between formality and informality, between graciousness and slap-happy.

Boy, oh boy! She was going to like it here. Sandra would be green with envy when she heard about it. Or would she? Sandra liked the gay life, plenty of boys, and there were no boys here. Not even Bruce's imaginary brother. Her hopes that Bruce might have a brother had been short-lived. He was an only child. Not that she minded really. She had only been telling herself a fairy tale. After all, if there had been a brother, he probably would not have been like Bruce; he would have been like all the other young men from whom she had been so anxious to escape.

'I must write to Sandra.' She went across to the writing desk. There was no need to go for her own writing pad. Envelopes, headed notepaper, even stamps, were there at her disposal. Everything laid on! She armed herself with blotter, writing paper and envelope and settled herself before the fire. *Dear Sandra*, she began. *It's simply super . . .*

CHAPTER FIVE

It was barely light the next morning when Beverley was roused by subdued sounds from the adjoining room. Somebody was raking out the fire. She lay and listened, listened to the closing of the door, wondered whether she ought to get up, what she ought to do about breakfast. She had not thought about it last night, she had merely accepted the intimation that it would be served in her room. Anyhow, there was no need to move yet, she would not be expected to be up too early on Sunday morning. She lay and watched as daylight gradually filled the room—she had drawn the curtains aside before she got into bed last night—glorying in the comfortable bed; that, at least, was modern—it was a really super spring mattress—studying the various items of furniture which made this room the most attractive she had ever slept in. She had still not ventured as far as putting a foot out of bed when there was a knock at the door.

'Come in.' To her dismay it was Matthew who entered.

'I hope you don't mind my bringing your tea, miss,' said the old man. 'Florence is always busy at this time and she said it was quite all right for me to do it, seeing as I am a grandfather.'

'Are you a grandfather, then, Matthew?'

'Yes, five times over,' said the old man proudly. He deposited the tray on the bedside table. 'Will it be all right if I bring your breakfast up in half an hour's time? The fire is going nicely now.' .

Beverley lay and gloated. She felt that she had not told Sandra half of it. She had never had morning tea in bed before. She revelled in the luxury of it. It was not that she was specially keen on tea at that hour, but the implication behind it, this fresh indication of the lady's life which was to be hers, tickled her fancy, flattered her ego. Even if she had hated morning tea, and she did not, she would still have persisted with the habit. It was one of the perquisites of her new status.

She was kneeling in front of the blazing fire when Matthew brought in her breakfast tray. He placed it on a small table.

'If there is anything you want, miss, will you ring?'

'Oh, I'm sure I shall not want anything else.' One glance at the tray had shown Beverley that breakfast was living up to the standard of everything else. The very sight of the tray made her hungry. There were grapefruit, a dish containing bacon, eggs, kidney, mushrooms—she would never be able to eat half of it, but luckily it was on a serving dish and she could have as much as she wanted—toast, butter, marmalade, all flanked by a pot of coffee and a jug of hot milk.

'Will you be going to church, miss? Will you want the car? The family, I believe, are not going this morning. Mr. Sheavyn's rheumatism is not too good and Mr. Bruce said they would not be going.'

Taken to church in a car! Beverley nearly said 'yes', just for the sheer joy of the experience, but she looked beyond the window. The sun was shining, it was a heavenly morning. It would be much pleasanter to walk.

'How far is it to church?' she asked.

'About three miles, miss.'

Beverley hesitated. Three miles was quite a step, and there would be three miles back again. She had not done much walking since she had been in London and would be out of practice. Once more she looked through the window. It would do her good and also help to pass the time.

'I think I will walk if you will tell me how to get there,' she said. Matthew's instructions were very clear and Beverley thoroughly enjoyed her walk to church. She had never been in the country at this time of the year and the autumn colours in this well-wooded district were a revelation to her. The service, the simplicity of the country church, enhanced the feeling of peace which seeped through the whole of her being; the homeward three miles were no more arduous than the outward ones had been. When she arrived at the dinner table, Beverley, conscious of a well-spent morning, was more than ready for the Sunday dinner which she felt sure would surpass any other Sunday dinner she had ever eaten.

'Matthew tells me that you walked to church.' It was Bruce Sheavyn who spoke. 'It is quite a walk there and back. Are you fond of walking?'

'Yes.' Beverley put down her soup spoon—the soup had been delicious. 'But I have not done much since I have lived in London.'

'Well, you will be able to get plenty of it here, but if you want to see the Lakes you will want something more than your own legs. Do you know the Lakes?'

'No, I have never been further north than Stratford before.'

'You will certainly have to see them while you are here—and in all weathers and seasons. There is no time when they have not got their own special beauty. They are glorious at present. The autumn tints have to be seen to be believed.' Bruce was an ardent devotee.

'The autumn colours here are lovely.' Beverley thought she would have to go far to surpass this morning's beauty.

'Yes, they are, but the Lakes are much grander. You didn't bring a cycle with you, did you?'

'No, I sold my cycle when I went to live in London.' Beverley repressed a tremor of amusement as she thought of her old cycle, the cycle which she had used for cycling to school ever since she was eleven. She had been ashamed of it for the last three years of her school life and had readily consigned it to the scrap-heap before she went to London.

'Do you by any chance drive a car?'

'No, I'm afraid not. It was hardly worth learning to drive in London, especially as there was no prospect of my owning a car for years.'

'No, I suppose not. Still, it is rather a pity. There is a spare car here which you would have been welcome to use.'

'I . . .' Cora Sheavyn had remained silent during this interchange. Whatever she had been about to say she thought better of it. 'Perhaps I could drive you sometimes,' she said. It was obviously a second thought.

Bruce looked at his wife in surprise. Cora rarely put herself out for anybody and he had certainly not expected her to do so for his young librarian. Had Beverley been the young man they had anticipated he might have understood it, but for a young girl! It did not ring true. He could not help wondering if Cora had some ulterior purpose though what it might be he could not imagine.

'Dash it,' he said to himself. 'Why must I always be suspicious. Why can't I take her at face value?' but he knew it was because life with Cora had taught him to be that way. Even as he thought it he tried to find some authentic reason for his wife's unwonted pleasantness. Could it be that the girl's youth and innocence appealed to her, awakened her motherly attributes? For Cora, even though she refused to have a child of her own, was surely not completely devoid of these. Her attitude to her brother, her junior by many years, was more that of a mother than a sister. Gilbert, Bruce had often thought, was the one person whom Cora had ever really loved.

It was the first reaction, suspicion, which had been the true one. It was no feeling of motherliness towards the girl which had prompted Cora's offer. Though she did not care enough about her husband to be troubled by ordinary jealousy, she was determined that nothing should happen that might imperil her position as the future mistress of Willerton

Grange. When she heard that Bruce had engaged a woman she knew that there might be a possibility of trouble. Bruce had never shown any signs of straying, but a designing woman in the house might alter that state of affairs. She did not have to be many minutes in Beverley's company to know that here was no designing woman, but she had come to see that there might be another danger. Hero-worship on the girl's part might prove just as much of a snare for her husband's affections.

Cora had no doubts about her ability to deal with this. She could, of course, make the place too hot for the girl to stay, but that would only involve another, and probably more unsatisfactory, appointment. It was very unlikely that a man would be obtainable. No, Cora told herself, I must first of all work to win the girl's affection for myself. Once that was accomplished, and she felt confident of being able to do that, she knew herself to be sufficiently a master of the art of denigration, of gentle insinuation, to counteract any tendency to hero-worship. It was with this in mind that she made the suggestion that the girl should accompany her in the car sometimes.

'Thank you.' For some reason which she could not explain Beverley did not view the prospect with undiluted pleasure. She felt that she would much rather walk than spend hours in the company of Cora Sheavyn in spite of the fact that Cora had shown nothing but friendliness to her. She was glad that since Bruce was at home she would not have to avail herself of the offer this afternoon.

As the sun still shone after dinner she decided to go for another walk. Once she started work, she thought, there would probably be little enough time for walks. She elected to go to the Knott, if she could find it, the knoll which Matthew had pointed out the previous day. It proved to be no difficult task; she soon discovered a signpost directing her there. She strolled gently up and up, traversing a path which, for the most part, was cut out of a pinewood. There were pine trees above her, pine trees stretching below. She reached a small clearing where a seat was strategically placed to command a fine view of the surrounding country. She sat down, glad to rest her feet after the unaccustomed exercise.

'It's a lovely view, isn't it?'

She turned round to find Bruce Sheavyn standing behind her. He had come from the opposite direction.

'Lovely,' she agreed.

'Not so lovely as it used to be,' Bruce's plaint, as he sat down beside her was the same as Matthew's had been. 'When I was younger, there were none of these houses and bungalows—at least very few. No, Arnside is not what it was. The only place that has not changed is the front, and that is awash with cars in the season. Oh, and the cove. That's changed, but it is a change for the better as far as I am concerned. They have made the cove—it used to be a children's paradise for climbing—into a yachting harbour. To my joy, I must confess.'

'Have you got a yacht?'

'Yes, a beauty. I must take you out sometimes. Do you like yachting?'

'I have never been on a yacht,' she confessed.

'We'll have to remedy that when the yachting season starts again. Yachting is the one thing we all enjoy. My grandfather and Cora as well as myself. I hope you will be another yachting fan.'

'I hope I shall.' Did his words mean that he expected her still to be here in the spring? Beverley had no idea how long this job was going to take but she had not envisaged it taking so long.

'Well, I think we had better be moving. I shall not be popular with my wife if I am not back for four o'clock tea.'

They walked back through the woods, going in the direction from which Bruce had come, walking at times among fallen leaves brilliantly coloured in all possible tones of yellow, orange, red. At other times their feet sank into a soft carpet of old pine needles. It was all new to the girl, all delightful. She felt that she could have gone on walking for ever, but Cora's four o'clock tea loomed like a spectre in their path.

'Would you join us for tea, Miss Gordon?' asked Bruce as they reached the house.

'I should like to very much.'

'Right. Just knock on the door at the opposite end of the corridor from yours. Come down as soon as you are ready.'

Entering the left wing was like stepping into another world. Even as she passed through the small vestibule, Beverley was struck by the contrast between it and the corridor along which she had come, but she nearly blinked— with amazement, with the whiteness—when she entered the spacious sitting-room. At first glimpse it was all white—white walls, white paint, the Indian carpet was white except for a pastel-coloured motif in the centre. Even the outsize suite was upholstered in white leather. Too much white, thought Beverley. The only relief was given by scattered brilliantly coloured cushions, two gargoyle-like dolls, brightly dressed, lolling in either corner of the big settee, and a very modern painting on one of the walls. The girl felt that the whole effect was funereal. Why funereal? Black was the mourning colour, not white. Then she remembered that white was the colour for mourning in China. She understood that now. There was something dead about all this whiteness.

'Come and sit by the fire, Miss Gordon.' Bruce rose from his chair and pulled one of the white-clothed monstrosities—that was how it struck her—close to the fire.

'How do you like your tea, Miss Gordon?' Cora held the teapot suspended in the air. 'No, I can't go on calling you Miss Gordon. Beverley, isn't it? Do you mind if we call you Beverley?' She knew that it would come sooner or later. Better from her than from Bruce, she decided.

'No. I should like it.'

'Right then, Beverley it is. Beverley, Bruce and Cora. B.B.C.! We ought to be able to do an act with that combination,' she laughed. 'Do you sing?' she asked the girl.

'No. Not a note, I'm afraid.'

'Oh, I had been hoping you would. Arnside has got a choir which I should like to join but I have nobody to go with. Bruce has just about as much voice as an old crow.'

'I never can think why you need somebody to go with,' objected her husband. 'You go to

91

those flower arrangement classes by yourself.'

'That's different. By the way, Beverley, how do you like my flower arrangements?'

Beverley hesitated. She had already noticed them scattered about the room. There was one on the small table facing her to which she had found her eyes returning time and time again, wondering what it was meant to be. It consisted of two white flowers, what sort of flowers Beverley could not have said, and a tortuous arrangement of bare twigs. The other arrangements were similar. There was not a hint of colour amongst the lot.

'Don't try to be polite, Beverley. Cora's flower arrangements are like modern art. One has to be educated to them.'

'And you are uneducable,' retorted his wife.

'I grant you that. I acknowledge that I am a Philistine where all this is concerned. Not that I don't appreciate some of your arrangements. Those leaf arrangements you did the other day were beautiful, but this arrangement of a few measly, colourless flowers and a lot of sticks just gets me.'

'Oh, you're hopeless.' It seemed for a moment that Cora's good humour was going to crack, but she made a quick recovery. 'Do try one of these little cakes, Beverley. I have got a marvellous cook at the moment. Long may she continue. Bruce, do ring for some more hot water, there's a pet.'

The entry of a neatly uniformed maid added one more to the list of anachronisms which Beverley had seen that afternoon. This room had struck her as being completely at odds with the house, the maid seemed to be equally at odds with the room. She would have been more at one with the service in the main part of the house, but there Matthew was the only one who conformed to the one-time idea of uniformed service. Florence was far too busy to trouble about it and the only other help she had, apart from her husband, was given by daily labour and the women who supplied this, like all their fellows, wore whatever suited them. Beverley had thought uniformed maids a thing of the past. Probably my ignorance, she thought. Maybe, if Mr. Sheavyn had a wife, there would be uniformed maids in the main building.

Conversation flowed easily. Beverley found that she was enjoying herself. There was only one thing that bothered her. She had to satisfy herself that the overheard conversation with its sinister sound had referred to an animal. She must get the conversation round to animals. It came quite easily. Life in the country and its amenities was a natural topic.

'Do you ride?' she asked Cora. If she discovered that either of them did ride, it would only be the next step to find out if one of the horses was old or disabled.

'No, I've never tried. Bruce used to but you haven't done much since we've been married, have you?'

'No, my leg's a bit of a nuisance at times, but I still do ride. I have only got one horse now. She's tip-top. I'll show you her someday soon.'

So horses were out, thought the girl. That left a dog or a cat. There were no signs of either but perhaps they were banished to the kitchen, or even kept outdoors.

'Haven't you got a cat or a dog?' she asked next, looking round as though she thought one might suddenly materialise. 'I thought all country people had pets.'

'We had, but we haven't got any now.' Bruce spoke rather stiffly.

'I'm not really keen on animals,' explained Cora. An understatement, thought her husband though he did not say anything.

'Oh.' Beverley felt deflated. She had been so certain that she had found the solution. She must not let them think there was any purpose behind her questions. 'I always wanted a puppy but my mother would not hear of it. She was like you,' she told Cora. 'She did not like animals.'

When she got up to go, Beverley felt that

her first visit to the young people's quarters had gone off very satisfactorily—except for the fact that she was further than ever from a solution to her problem. Still, that had nothing to do with the satisfactoriness of the visit. As far as she could see, the only way in which she might have fallen short was in her inability to address Cora by her Christian name. 'Bruce' had come easily to her lips, but she had been unable to bring out the word 'Cora'. Bruce's wife seemed so much older though it was not only this that made the difficulty. She had called women older than Cora by their Christian names. Whatever it was, there was something about Cora Sheavyn which, in spite of her friendly attitude, made the word 'Cora' stick in her throat.

Yesterday she had wondered how on earth Bruce Sheavyn could have brought himself to marry this woman. Today she understood how it could have been possible. She realised that Cora Sheavyn, given the will, would be able to charm most men—for a time. Perhaps it was because she was herself a woman that the charm did not work fully, that she still had reservations, that she still thought Bruce Sheavyn worthy of something better in the way of a wife. Or was it just that she thought Cora Sheavyn too old for him?

'Well, young lady, are you ready to take me

on with that game of chess?' It was these words which heralded the last phase of what had been for Beverley an unexpectedly social day. Favourable though her impressions had been on the previous evening she had certainly not expected that her first day at Willerton Grange would be quite so enjoyable. She, who had anticipated feeling like the ugly duckling thrown into that alien nest, now likened herself to a stray kitten which had been whole-heartedly adopted into a family. As the day progressed, she had become more and more convinced that she had been fantastically lucky when she had seen that advertisement in the *Sunday Telegraph*. It seemed incredible that it should have occurred just at this time. Her session in John Sheavyn's apartment added yet another stone to the edifice of happiness which had been building up all day.

'I have enjoyed that.' It was just after eleven o'clock when John Sheavyn pushed the chessboard to one side. 'You are a worthy opponent, my dear. They taught you well at that school of yours. I would like another game but there is no saying how long it would go on and you have got to work tomorrow if I have not.' He began to gather up the ivory pieces, placing them in their box. 'I'm just going to have a glass of whisky myself, but I don't suppose you are one of these young ladies who drink whisky.'

'No, I'm not.'

'That's right. I'm glad you are not. I suppose I'm a square, as they say these days, but I don't like girls who toss off their drinks just like the men. I suppose you might say "Why shouldn't they?", and I couldn't say why, but I don't like it. Anyhow you are not one of them so why am I blethering? Good night, my dear,' he patted her shoulder, 'and thank you for the game. We will have another before long.'

Up in her bedroom Beverley reviewed the day just past, thought of the days ahead. If only it could keep on as it had begun. And there was no reason why it should not. Surely the first days would be the most difficult. She gave a sigh of complete contentment as she gave one last look round before she drew back her bedroom curtains. She gazed into the darkness beyond. How dark it was here. In London it was never really dark, here only one or two distant lights pierced the night's velvet curtain. Otherwise it was complete darkness. No, not complete. Below her she saw a slow-moving speck. She opened her window quietly and craned out. There was the sound of footsteps. A curtain was pulled aside at a downstairs window. The shaft of light revealed the walker's identity. It was Bruce

Sheavyn—smoking a cigarette or a pipe. She could not tell which.

'Good night, Bruce,' she whispered, but too low for him to hear. Silently she pulled the window to. That last glimpse of her employer added just that final touch to her contentment. Life is good, she thought as she snuggled down between the sheets.

CHAPTER SIX

Life continued to be good. Beverley slipped into the new setting as easily as a ball into an oiled socket. She came no nearer to solving the question of those threatening words, but was convinced that there was some innocent meaning. The more she knew of Bruce Sheavyn the more convinced she was that it could not be otherwise, but the more she knew of his wife the less easy she found it to respond sincerely to her gestures of friendship. Respond she must, though, as far as lay in her power. Unless she responded in some measure, her stay at Willerton Grange would be very short-lived. She was only too aware of this, aware that she must not alienate this woman, who she had to admit had shown her nothing but kindness. It was Cora who was responsible for the fact that Beverley's working day was so different from the one she had mapped out for herself.

'Bruce,' Cora had tackled her husband at dinner on the first Monday night, 'do you expect your librarian to work office hours?'

'Hey?' Bruce looked up from his plate. 'What do you mean? What are you talking about?'

'What I say. Do you expect Beverley to work from nine to one, from two till six?'

'I most certainly do not. It is not that sort of a job.'

'Well, that is what she is doing, and only taking the minimum time off for morning coffee and afternoon tea.' She caught the questioning look in her husband's eye. 'I know about the coffee and tea because I popped in to make sure she wasn't forgotten, and she herself told me she intended to work office hours.'

'Is that so, Beverley?'

'Yes.' She knew that Bruce Sheavyn was only referring to her office hours, but it was also true that his wife had made an appearance in the library at eleven o'clock and again at four, ostensibly to assure herself that morning coffee and afternoon tea had been brought there. As though Matthew would be likely to forget, Beverley had thought. The house was run on such well-oiled wheels that she could not imagine any guest or employee being forgotten.

'That's foolish, Beverley. It is too intensive a job to be treated in that way. Remember, in an office, there are always comings and goings to break the monotony. There are other people about. If you put in six hours a day here that should be quite enough. And choose your hours to suit yourself. I suggest that when the weather is decent you take the time off in the afternoon, go for a walk or something then. There is no chance of getting out after tea at this time of the year. Do your second stint between tea and dinner, if you like. By the way, when I say six hours a day I mean a five-day week. If you do thirty hours a week that is the maximum that I expect.'

'I don't really feel that is enough,' protested Beverley.

'And I say it is,' smiled her employer. 'You can space it as you like, work Saturdays and Sundays if you like, but you are not to work more than the thirty hours. I am not a slave driver.'

So Beverley found herself with quite an amount of free time on her hands, free time which—when it was possible—she spent in the open air, exploring the country, learning to love it. Her work, too, when she had overcome the initial confusion, was interesting and congenial. When she had entered the library on that first morning, she had just stood and stared. Where did she begin? She walked round and round the room, looking at everything, getting her bearings. She studied the old library of books, their positioning, their grouping, sorting the books scattered on the floor. This was no task which could be approached in a haphazard way. There had to be a plan. She counted her shelves, numbered them, made a list of all the subjects of which she could think, allotted shelves to each subject. Then she started to work on the books of the old library, moving them to their correct places in her new listing. By the end of that first day, she felt that she had something to show for her labours. What was more, she knew where she was going. When she had finally got all the books into their respective categories—she had not the slightest idea how long that would take her— then she would be able to start on what she considered to be the real librarian work.

She had been at Willerton Grange for about ten days when Bruce asked her if she would care to go into Kendal with him the next day. She had been for a couple of drives with Cora, but they had only been in the country.

'I am only going in for the half day tomorrow,' he said. 'It would give you a break, give you a chance to see Kendal without having too much time to fill in, and you could come back with me for lunch.'

Needless to say, Beverley accepted the offer. She had toyed with the idea of taking the bus into Kendal in the near future, but this would be a much pleasanter way. The work was going well, but it was necessarily a solitary

102

occupation and she did not altogether appreciate the breaks which did occur—the occasions when Cora Sheavyn invaded her privacy. A morning spent away from the house would provide a change and the fact that part of it was to be spent in Bruce's company added to the attractiveness of the proposal. The more she saw of Bruce Sheavyn the more she liked him.

She had expected to enjoy the drive into Kendal, but it proved even more pleasurable than she had anticipated. Conversation flowed between them as naturally as water from a spring. She had thought that the scenery they passed through would be one of the attractions of the ride, but after the first few miles, she hardly noticed it. Though it was now November, the trees still blazed with glory. 'If we get a cold snap,' Bruce told her, 'we shall soon see a difference.' But the beauty of the trees, the newness of the route, were soon completely forgotten. She was too engrossed in conversation to give more than a passing glance to her surroundings.

'How is it that your family has a factory?' she asked at one stage. 'I thought all old families lived on the proceeds of their estates, that they scorned trade of any kind. And yours is an old family, isn't it?'

'It is. We are certainly an old family. There

have been Sheavyns at Willerton Grange—or rather at the house which stood on the same site—since the fifteenth century. The old house was partly demolished by fire in the time of George II and after that, the present one was built, but we have owned the property since the fifteenth century, as I said.'

'And yet you go daily to business, and your grandfather used to do likewise.'

'Yes, and his grandfather before him. We can't afford to have any false pride about trade. A good many of my ancestors were definitely rakes, at least they let their money go through their hands like water through a sieve. Not only their money, but their lands. Their gambling debts kept chewing off bits of land until the estate was reduced to what it is at present—and that is just the house, the garden and the nearby parkland. Fortunately there came along a Sheavyn who not only refused to gamble away the last bit, but also decided that steps must be taken to earn money if he was going to hang on to what he had still got. So he borrowed money to build Sheavyn's factory just outside Kendal and he managed to make a go of it. And it has been Sheavyn's factory which has kept us going ever since.'

'Do you like the work?' asked Beverley curiously.

'Yes, I do. I don't say there wasn't a time

when I thought I would like to be something else—I had ideas about going in for engineering—but after my accident this was not only the easiest proposition but I had realised how much it meant to my grandfather. I find now that I really enjoy it. You know, there is a lot to be said for these old family businesses. There is such a friendly, homely spirit in the place. I only hope we shall manage to keep it as it is and never get involved in one of those take-over bids.'

'Don't you approve of those big concerns? Don't they mean that businesses can be run more economically and more efficiently?'

'They probably do, but there are other things to life besides economy and efficiency. At least I think so. I grant you that competition is cut-throat, that Britain is up against it, but nevertheless I think there is a place for the small firms. You lose all humanity in these tremendous combines and I also think you get inferior work. The men are just out for what they can get. There is no sense of loyalty, of being part of a family, as there is in our business, for instance.'

Egged on by Beverley he went on to talk of his ideas and ideals. The girl listened entranced. She could hardly believe it possible that they could already be in Kendal when Bruce pulled the car up at the side of the pavement.

'This is Highgate,' he said. 'I will leave you to roam about as you like. You can just snoop around, if you prefer it, shop gaze if that is in your line, or, again, if you are interested, there's a museum at the end of the town. It's all yours! I will be back at this spot at half past twelve.'

The next three hours Beverley spent in exploring the old town, going through the arches which led off the main street, finding herself in tiny lanes or alleys with houses on either side, houses with gardens which, in the spring, would be bright with flowers. She wandered down to the river Kent, the river which, so Bruce had told her, quite often overflowed into the streets of Kendal. She shop-gazed, but not for long. After London shops, these offered little and she had soon exhausted their contents. She did think of going to the museum, it might be interesting, but she decided to save it for the possible wet day. Today, the only time she spent indoors was when she went for her morning coffee. She was so afraid of being late for her appointment with Bruce that she landed at the meeting place with a quarter of an hour to spare. There was nothing for it but to spend that last fifteen minutes pacing up and down Highgate, looking at shops which had lost

106

what little allure they might have had.

The drive home was as delightful, passed as quickly as had the journey into Kendal. It seemed to the girl that she had known Bruce for years, so easy were they together. Was being with Bruce like being with a brother? she wondered in her ignorance. Did brothers feel the ease and comfort with each other that she felt with Bruce Sheavyn?

It was that evening that Cora Sheavyn made the suggestion that she should teach Beverley to drive.

'How did you enjoy your morning in Kendal?' They had only just sat down to dinner when she fired her question.

'Very much.'

'Well, it would be a change. I should get completely mouldy if I lived the life you do.' She turned to her husband. 'Bruce,' she said, 'Beverley ought to learn to drive. She can't be about here all day and all evening, and that's what it amounts to now the winter is here. She will be completely house-bound in the evenings.'

'I don't mind,' protested Bevereley. 'I could get a bus if I wanted to,' she said, feeling distinctly uncomfortable. 'After all, I had a good idea what it would be like when I came, but it has been a lot nicer than I imagined. I'm really quite content. And, as for the evenings,

I play chess with Mr. Sheavyn several evenings a week.'

'And very much I enjoy that, Beverley, but a young lady needs other diversions than playing chess with an old fellow like me.'

'Yes, Grandfather, I agree with you. If I were you, Beverley, I should avail myself of Cora's offer. It is a good one, and I rather think it will be a pleasure to Cora, won't it, dear?' he asked his wife.

'Yes.' Cora glanced at her husband, suspecting an ulterior meaning behind these words—surely he had no idea why she had made the suggestion—but there was no sign of guile, her husband's face told her that the words simply meant what they said. 'It will give me something to do. I find the days boring if Beverley doesn't.'

'Accept the offer, Beverley.' Bruce did not give his wife time to enlarge on her boredom.

'Thank you, I will.' Beverley did not know that those simple words were to open a gate on the memory of the first words she had ever heard in Cora Sheavyn's voice.

'A very good idea,' agreed John Sheavyn. 'Every young person ought to be able to drive.' He turned to Beverley. 'Did you ever hear that tale about the young man who wanted to take his fiancée for a drive?'

'No, I don't think so.' Beverley was pretty

sure that she would not have heard it. Funny tales had not made a practice of coming her way in the past.

'That is a new one on me too, Grandfather, I think.'

'I expect it is. I only heard it when I was in Kendal last week. Well, as I was saying, there was a young man who...' He proceeded to tell the tale with all the artistry which came so naturally to him. Even Cora's face slipped when he came to the denouement. Emboldened by his success John Sheavyn produced several more tales during the course of the meal, each fitting aptly in with the conversation, one other of them being new to his grandson, all of them new to Beverley, and to Cora, though she would not have acknowledged it, but she did give a grudging applause. It was the first time Beverley had seen the old man in such good form. Chess was too serious a game to allow of much in the way of humorous tales and Beverley usually departed as soon as the last game was finished.

The course of driving lessons began the next day, but was brought to an abrupt, if temporary, halt on the third day. Though it was still early in November, so early that everyone gloomily predicted it to be the beginning of a severe winter, not only was there a severe frost, but there was also a heavy snowfall. To Beverley, accustomed to the unpleasantness of snow in London, the fall of snow transformed the scene into one which might have stepped straight out of the pages of a fairy tale book. The sun shone on a dazzling whiteness which was natural and beautiful, not like the whiteness of Cora's sitting-room. The trees were no longer a riot of colour, their branches were laden with a new foliage, a white foliage which had the ephemeral quality that might cause it to vanish in a day—a strong sun or a sudden rise in temperature, either might cause it to dissolve into nothingness, but while it lasted it was infinitely beautiful. Beverley borrowed a pair of Florence's Wellingtons and plunged into the thick snow. Cora stayed in and hugged the fire.

The severe weather lasted only a few days but that was long enough to lay the finger of winter on the land. When the snow went it took with it all the colour which had given the landscape such a charm. Now, the only colour—as far as nature was concerned—came from the dark green of the evergreens, the dull green of the winter grass, sometimes the blue of the sky, but even that blue was faded, washed out by nature's own detergent.

Cora re-started the driving lessons as soon as the snow had cleared. Every day, unless the weather was too unpleasant, and though it was a November which had more than its share of good days, there were yet those of gales and continual rain, Beverley would be called upon to leave her work in the library in order to have her lesson. Cora was enthusiastic about her pupil's progress, declared her to be a natural driver. The girl, herself, felt less certain of her prowess and though she enjoyed the actual driving and was grateful for the help, she often wished that she had some other teacher, someone who was herself more steady and reliable, and, above all, one who was not so addicted to resting her hand on Beverley's, who was not quite so generous with her gestures of appreciation. Beverley not only felt that she could dispense with these, but she was at a loss how to receive them, to know how much was really meant by them. She was delighted when Matthew offered to give her some lessons.

'When Mrs. Bruce is out, of course,' he had said.

'Aye, you'd better not let that one see you doing it.'

Florence Benson made no secret of her dislike for Cora Sheavyn as Beverley knew by now. Latterly she had formed the habit of taking her morning coffee in the kitchen. It had come about quite simply. There had been a morning during the cold spell when

Matthew had limped badly when he brought up Beverley's breakfast.

'What is the matter, Matthew?' she had asked. 'Have you hurt your leg?'

'It's the rheumatism, Miss Beverley.' The formal Miss Gordon had very soon been banished from the kitchen. 'I'm like the master. The rheumatism gives me gyp at times, and today is one of them.'

As it neared eleven o'clock that morning Beverley decided to bring her own coffee from the kitchen, to save Matthew that one unnecessary journey.

'It's good of you, Miss Beverley, but you need not have bothered, I could have brought it.'

'Why should you when I have got a perfectly good pair of legs?' Beverley looked round the kitchen. 'What a smashing kitchen you have got, Florence,' she exclaimed.

'Yes, I have,' agreed the woman. Her face beamed with pride. 'Mr. Sheavyn told me to get just what I wanted and to have the place decorated to suit myself. So I chose the pale green and cream and, though I say it myself, I think you'd go a long way before you'd find a prettier kitchen.'

'I think so too, Florence. And you have got everything.' She wandered round the room, inspecting the equipment, the eye-level gas stove, the Aga cooker, the automatic washer, the luxurious refrigerator. She did not know much about kitchens, she had never been allowed to be domesticated, but even with her small knowledge she realised that this was the type of kitchen which was advertised in the magazines as 'your dream kitchen'.

'Yes, I've got everything,' Florence said complacently. 'And I've got the best master anyone ever had. And Mr. Bruce is just such another. It's a damned shame he ever married that woman.'

'Florence!' Beverley did not know whether the warning note was meant as a reproof for the word or the sentiment.

'Well, it is, and what's the good of wrapping it up? If Miss Beverley don't know already that the woman's a bitch she soon will.'

'Florence!' Once more Matthew tried to restrain his wife.

'Oh, you and your Florence,' exclaimed the woman. She turned to Beverley. 'I suppose you wouldn't care to have your cup of coffee with us. We're just going to have one and you'd be welcome if you liked.'

'Florence!' said Matthew once more. The old man was a stickler for etiquette but Beverley interrupted before he could voice his objection.

'I should like to.' She accepted the offer

with real gratitude. She liked both Matthew and his bustling, outspoken wife. In spite of her denial, that she found the days long, there were times when she felt the need to speak to somebody, someone other than Cora.

That morning set a pattern for future mornings. Matthew no longer brought a tray of coffee to the library for Beverley to consume in solitary state. She now went along to the kitchen and enjoyed her morning coffee in the company of these two kindly people. Matthew's offer to add to her quota of driving lessons was only one of the many kindnesses which she received from their hands. She had been doubtful at one time as to whether Bruce might disapprove of this new arrangement. She was quite certain that Cora would, but she saw no reason why the latter should ever know; Cora no longer timed her visits for eleven o'clock, but she did tell Bruce.

'A very good idea,' he had said. 'You must get a bit lonely at times and you could not come across a nicer, more genuine couple than Matthew and Florence.'

So Beverley became a regular kitchen visitor, a ready listener to Florence's tales of her two children, of John—named after Mr. Sheavyn, you can be sure—who had become an engineer, of Margaret who had been a teacher before her marriage. She admired the photographs of the grandchildren, commiserated over the fact that they were so far away that their grandparents saw them only seldom. She came to look upon the old couple as real friends. Matthew's offer to add to her driving lessons was not altogether unexpected. She was aware that he had not a very high idea of her present tutor's capabilities.

'I've told Mr. Bruce I'm going to give you a few lessons,' he told her one morning.

'What did he say? Did he approve?'

'Yes, he said it would certainly be a help, that it would probably give you a greater sense of security, as though Mrs. Bruce is a competent driver she was also highly strung.'

'That's one way of saying it,' broke in Florence as she took the pan of hot milk off the stove. 'I suppose he could hardly say that his wife was a bitch.'

'Florence!'

'Oh, you're too good for this world.' She placed a cup of coffee in front of her husband and planted a kiss on the top of his white head. 'You'd never say a word against anyone. I believe in calling a spade a spade.'

'And a bitch a bitch,' murmured Matthew with one of his rare touches of humour.

And bitch was really the word, thought Beverley, remembering Cora's conversation

115

in the car the previous afternoon, and on several other occasions. It had appeared to the girl lately that Cora was not so much concerned with teaching her to drive as with inculcating her with a distrust and dislike of Cora's husband. For the most part, these attempts at disillusionment were hardly more than insinuations so insidious that afterwards it was difficult to pinpoint them, but there were other times when she treated the girl to diatribes on men in general and her husband in particular.

'You be sensible and give the men a wide berth,' she warned her. She made a show of the older, wiser woman giving of her experience to the young and innocent. 'They are all alike. I thought Bruce was different until I married him, but I soon found out he was just as bad as the rest of them. Ugh!' The shudder of disgust was not completely feigned since she was naturally a frigid woman.

'Yes.' Against her will Beverley found herself agreeing. It was so pat with her own limited experience, and yet she could not believe it to be true of Bruce. There was sufficient truth in Cora's words to carry conviction to an unprejudiced ear, but Beverley was already biased in Bruce's favour and antipathetic to Cora. Nevertheless, a certain amount of poison inevitably seeped through.

Yet another of Cora's more sledge-hammer tactics was her accusation of Bruce's infidelities.

'He thinks I don't know the real reason when he's late home, when he goes down to Arnside at night. Always an excuse but I'm not as green as that.'

Once again, Beverley discounted these charges, rightly putting them down to Cora's way of saying 'keep off the grass'. She need not have bothered, thought the girl indignantly, still hanging on to the fiction that she was not as other girls, I like him, but there's nothing of that in it.

It was only two or three days later when something occurred which made these problems appear trivial. Usually Beverley started her lesson immediately after lunch. They were generally back well before John Sheavyn set out on what he termed his daily constitutional. Occasionally Beverley had accompanied him. This afternoon Cora sent a message to say that she would not be ready until half an hour after the usual time.

The lesson went very smoothly. Cora was, as she could be occasionally, merely friendly and the girl had enjoyed the lesson. They had no sooner turned into the drive than Beverley saw John Sheavyn walking ahead of them.

'There's Mr. Sheavyn,' she said.

'Yes.'

Suddenly she felt Cora's hands on hers, turning the wheel, heading the car straight for the old man.

CHAPTER SEVEN

Only a miracle could have saved him, but somehow or other that miracle happened. How she had the strength, let alone the presence of mind, to wrench the wheel from Cora's grasp, she would never know. To wrench the wheel away, to change direction, to stamp her foot on the brake! But she did. The car slewed round and careered into the opposite hedge before it came to a dead stop. White and shaken, Beverley opened the car door and went across to John Sheavyn. Cora was instantly on her heels.

'Heavens, Beverley!' she cried out. 'What were you doing? It was a mercy I was there. You would have killed Mr. Sheavyn if I had not been there, if I had not managed to grab the wheel.'

So that was how she was going to play it. Beverley said nothing. What could she say? She certainly could not say that Cora Sheavyn had seized that wheel and deliberately turned it on her husband's grandfather.

'And I thought you were becoming such a good driver,' Cora said with just the right note of reproach. She turned to smile at the old man—a Judas smile, thought Beverley. 'I hope you didn't get too much of a shock, Mr. Sheavyn.'

'No, I'm all right. I was ready to skip aside,' but Beverley knew that no skipping aside could have saved him had the car continued on the course which Cora Sheavyn had intended. 'What went wrong, Beverley? Did you go into a skid? The road is a bit muddy.'

'I don't know what I did.' Beverley had realised by this time that the only course open to her was to play along with Cora, even to go further, to pretend to Cora. If Cora knew that Beverley was fully aware of what had happened, then Beverley would certainly have to pay for the knowledge, of that she was sure, though she did not have any idea what form that payment would take. Her only way would be to equal Cora in duplicity, to pretend that she did not know what had happened, that she thought the fault had been hers, and that it was Cora's hands on hers which had diverted the car and averted tragedy.

The near tragedy posed yet another problem for the girl, bringing back as it did the words which had first informed her of Cora's existence. According to those, her husband was also a party to any attempt at murder, but if she could not believe Bruce capable of killing at all, still less could she credit that he would connive at any plot to kill the grandfather of whom he was so obviously fond. It just did not make sense. She tried to remember exactly what those words were, to find some loophole—or whether they had applied to John Sheavyn and Cora's action that afternoon certaintly indicated that they did.

'I'll kill him myself if you don't get a move on.' Mentally she heard the words again, heard Bruce's reply. 'I tell you I will do it, but in my own time.' She was sure those words were the right ones. She had said them over to herself so often, trying to find a meaning for them. She tried again in the light of the afternoon's occurrence and this time fresh light came to her. Even if those words did apply to his grandfather, it did not mean that Bruce was a party to his grandfather's murder. He would probably rate those words of Cora's as merely hot air. Cora obviously wanted him to do something to the old man, make him do something or other, but Bruce refused to be hurried. What it could be she had no idea, but there was probably nothing sinister in it at all. Cora probably had not meant those words when she said them, though it was quite clear that she had come to mean them now.

It was very hard that evening when Cora gave her husband her version of the accident. It not only went against the grain to find herself unfairly put in the wrong before Bruce, but she also felt that she ought to warn John Sheavyn's grandson of the peril in which the old man stood. If Cora had tried to murder him once she would not scruple to try again—and next time she might succeed. Beverley found it most difficult to keep silent, and all the more so as Bruce Sheavyn did not seem altogether convinced that his wife had told the complete tale.

'What made Beverley go off at a tangent like that?' he asked when Cora had wrung every drop of drama out of the situation. 'Was it a skid? Was there a muddy patch there?'

'Search me!' Cora spread her hands wide, disclaiming knowledge and responsibility alike. 'I looked afterwards. It had been raining of course, but I couldn't see any special reason for a skid just there. I guess Beverley isn't quite as proficient as she thought she was, eh, Beverley?'

There was malice in the last words. Bruce looked at his wife. He had thought she was fond of Beverley. Was she tiring of her, was she making the most of this accident—his grandfather would have pushed it aside—in order to discredit Beverley? Was this the beginning of a crusade to undermine their confidence in the girl, to lead to her ultimate dismissal? He had seen too much of his wife's devious ways latterly. Love, or what he had taken to be love, had blinded him during the early days of his marriage, but love had disappeared, and with it, the blinkers which had obscured his mental view. In the first years of their marriage he had longed desperately for children, especially had he wanted a son to carry on the Sheavyn name and tradition. Now, he felt that he no longer cared. What guarantee was there that the child would not inherit its mother's twisted nature, its mother's lack of integrity. The name of Sheavyn might be perpetuated, but its connotation would possibly change lamentably. It would no longer stand for honour and uprightness. At least there was a tremendous risk that this would be the case. There were many times when he told himself this, others when he was equally convinced that the risk was no more than any sane man would take. But, whether he was willing or not was beside the point. This was a matter which required the co-operation of two people and Cora was still, as she had been from the outset, determined not to embarrass herself with a child.

Beverley was glad she was not playing chess that evening. It was possible that John Sheavyn might not mention the incident— surely there had been enough said already—

but the possibility could not be ruled out and the girl felt that she could not face any further discussion until she had had time to think about it quietly, to sum up all the implications, to consider all the future contingencies which might be involved, to review her own attitude, past, present and to come.

She was pretty nearly convinced that what had happened that afternoon was an attempt at murder and she was equally convinced, after seeing Bruce's reception of Cora's account, that he had no conception that murder had been intended even though he did not altogether accept his wife's version. He had no idea of it, but Beverley thought she knew now that Cora Sheavyn not only felt that she could murder the owner of Willerton Grange, she had every intention of doing so. Believing this to be so, was she, Beverley, doing right in letting her get away with it? Her mind went round and round, weighing the pros and cons, not only of Cora's behaviour, but also of her own. However she argued with herself that she ought to say what had really happened, she always came back to her first conclusion. She could convince no one. She might plant certain suspicions but even that was doubtful. Cora was clever. She would cause those suspicions to rebound on Beverley herself. To tell the truth would serve no useful purpose. It would merely result in her own dismissal. What employer could retain the services of someone who had falsely—so it would appear—accused his wife of intended murder? She poked the fire furiously, she had sat before that fire for what seemed ages, doing nothing, just thinking—thinking and thinking.

'No,' she said aloud, 'I've got to keep on as I have started.' For John Sheavyn's sake as well as her own, she decided. Most certainly for her own. In spite of all this she wanted to stay on at Willerton Grange. Except for Cora, it was perfection and she was determined not to let Cora spoil it for her. She did not pretend that it was for John Sheavyn's sake that she wanted to remain in his home, but she did tell herself that her presence might be, to a certain extent, a safeguard for him. She, alone, knew that he was in danger. It was no use saying that she could apprise others of that danger. She could not go round saying that Cora Sheavyn was a menace to the life of her husband's grandfather, but she could keep her eyes open, she could be on the alert in case Cora should strike again, as she almost certainly would.

The next morning added yet more fuel to her intention to avoid alienating Cora. When she arrived in the kitchen just before eleven o'clock, Jean Laver, Cora's maid, and her mother were just about to leave.

'And no character,' said the mother. 'I call it right-down wicked, that's what I do.'

'It is, but what else would you expect from her ladyship? I suppose you were telling the truth, Jean, when you said she nudged your elbow?' Florence Benson asked.

'Of course I was,' replied the girl indignantly. 'She nudged my elbow—and purposely—just as I was lifting the tray. She wanted to get rid of me.'

'Why?' Matthew would not let such a statement go unchallenged.

'She said,' the girl bridled, 'she said that I was making eyes at the master.'

'And were you?' Florence forestalled the older woman's stream of invective.

'Of course not.' The air of injured innocence sat ill. Beverley could well believe that as far as the accusation went, Cora had been in the right. She, herself, had noticed Jean's black eyes hard at work when her master was about. If they had failed to have any effect, it was not Jean's fault. Whether Cora's subsequent actions were equally justified was open to question.

'Did she give you notice because of the broken crockery?' Florence had listened to the

126

account Jean and her mother had given but now she was probing to find the whole truth. Much though she disliked Cora Sheavyn, Florence was not the person to accept a one-sided tale.

'No.' Jean spoke sullenly. 'I tell you, she knocked my elbow and the tray went crash. She started to carry on at me and I lost my temper. I turned on her and told her that she had done it on purpose.'

'You couldn't expect her to take that,' said Florence, struggling for fairness.

'But she was telling the truth,' protested the mother.

'I believe you, Mrs. Laver, but it doesn't always do to say everything that is true.'

No, it doesn't, thought Beverley. If I had told the truth yesterday, I should probably be like Jean Laver, out of a job. She listened as Florence shepherded mother and daughter out of the door, promising to do her best to get the girl another post.

'That girl ought to have had more sense than to go making eyes at the master,' she said as she came back, 'even though Mrs. Bruce is not a specially jealous woman. And goodness knows she has no reason to be. He never looks at another woman though the Lord knows why. Probably thinks the one he's got is more than enough. Anyhow Jean Laver ought to

127

have known she would not last long once she started that game. That woman is never at a loss in finding a way to get rid of someone she doesn't want. By the way, Miss Beverley, what's this about you trying to run over Mr. Sheavyn? Matthew said that's what Mrs. Bruce made it sound like last night.'

'I certainly did not try to run over Mr. Sheavyn.' Beverley remembered that Matthew had been in the dining-room when Cora had been giving her version of the happening. 'The car certainly did make for Mr. Sheavyn, but I don't know what made it swerve. Luckily it swerved again and avoided him.'

'And I can guess the name of somebody who would be sorry it did not continue on its course,' said Florence darkly. 'Matthew said Mrs. Bruce said it was she who tried to turn it aside. It's more than I can do to swallow that one. Think she'd lift a finger to save Mr. Sheavyn! Not she! She'd be far more likely to lift a finger the other way. I wouldn't put it beyond her having done so.' Florence looked at Beverley as though inviting her to bear out her words.

'Florence!' There was the old warning note. 'Miss Beverley has told us she doesn't know what happened.'

'U-um.' Florence looked as though she

128

could have said much more. Beverley felt strangely comforted. She had not given anything away, but undoubtedly Florence had her suspicions that all was not as had been reported. That meant that she was not the only one who knew of the danger to Mr. Sheavyn. She would not be single-handed in her fight to ensure the old gentleman's safety but the alliance would have to be secret, unacknowledged.

'But why should Mrs. Bruce want Mr. Sheavyn dead?' she asked. She could not think how the kindly old man could have aroused such a hatred in Cora Sheavyn.

'She wants to be the mistress of Willerton Grange, wants to have it all her own way, have her hands on the money. She thinks once the old gentleman's gone she'll be able to do what she wants. She thinks she'll be able to browbeat her husband into letting her have her own way just as she did when they first came here, but it's my guess she's got another think coming. She'll find Mr. Bruce has learnt something since then. Still, it'll be goodbye to us, Matthew, when the master's gone.'

'I know that,' agreed her husband.

'Not that I'd want to stay under that woman, not even if she went down on her bended knees to me. Not even if Mr. Bruce did.'

'Well, he won't.'

'No, I know he won't, but it's sorry I'll be to leave Mr. Bruce, but even for his sake I could not stick that woman.'

'Well, the master's not dead yet.' Matthew stirred his coffee vigorously. He did not like this subject. Deep down he felt that there was truth in his wife's inveighing and, likewise, deep down, he was troubled for his master's safety, but Matthew had never been a fighter, and he was certainly not one to go out to meet trouble. Rather he would refuse to face its possibility until such time as either it struck or, as he had hoped, bypassed him. 'Mrs. Bruce is going to her flower class this afternoon, isn't she?' He turned the subject.

'Yes.'

'Good. We'll get a lesson in. You could do with one after what happened yesterday.' He said no more about the accident, but Beverley felt that Florence was not the only one who thought that Cora, in some way, might lie at the root of the trouble.

As the days went by, Beverley began to feel that the incident might never have occurred. Life at Willerton Grange went smoothly along. Cora's attitude to Beverley seemed to have undergone very little change. Perhaps she was slightly less friendly but that could have been accounted for by the fact that in

130

early December, Beverley not only took her driving test, but passed it. There was no further need for those sessions in the car, sessions which the girl had learned to hate. There was consequently far less opportunity for Cora to instil her doses of poison. Beverley congratulated herself on having decided to shoulder the blame for the driving accident. The only trouble was that she was almost beginning to believe it was true.

As December brought a lessening in her contacts with Cora so it brought an increase in the times which she spent with Bruce.

He formed the habit of dropping into the library on the evenings when Beverley was working there. If she was not playing chess with John Sheavyn, she would quite often put in an hour or two there after dinner. Ostensibly Bruce had come in the first place to enquire as to her progress, to discuss the work with her, but the discussion on the library more often than not digressed into other matters, matters which had no connection with the library, not even with books. Their talks ranged over a diversity of subjects. Sometimes they agreed, sometimes not, but always there was a feeling of unity between them, a friendship which deepened and deepened as the days went by. Beverley did sometimes wonder what Cora's reactions to his frequent absences were. Did she think he had gone to Arnside, womanising? She did not think so. That had only been one of Cora's tales. He usually made a reference to the fact that his wife was watching television, but she knew that Cora was not always willing to accept that as an excuse for her husband's defection. She did not know that since her attempt on John Sheavyn's life, Cora had felt the need to tread carefully.

'Have you any plans for Christmas, Beverley?' he asked her on one of these evenings.

'N-no,' she hesitated. 'I have not decided anything yet.'

She was, in fact, troubled as to what she would do then. She had a letter from Sandra only two days ago, asking her to spend Christmas at her home as she had done the two previous Christmases, and until that letter she had not had the slightest doubt that it was there that she would spend Christmas. Sandra's letter, however, had contained news which made Beverley think again. 'Laurie and I became engaged last Sunday.' Sandra had written. Later on, speaking of the invitation for Christmas, she had said, 'Don't let my engagement make any difference to your coming for Christmas, will you? We shall want you just as much.' Beverley doubted the truth of that last statement. She did not doubt that Sandra thought she meant what she said, but since she had also said that Laurie was going home with her at Christmas, Beverley surmised that she would definitely be superfluous. Laurie would almost certainly feel any friend of Sandra very much *de trop*, and though Sandra might deny similar feelings, Beverley was equally sure that they would be there, however much the girl might try to stifle them. She had not yet answered Sandra's letter, but she had already made up her mind. Whatever else she did she was not going to spend Christmas with the Knight family.

Bruce did not pursue the subject further but he did decide in his own mind that Beverley should be asked to spend Christmas at Willerton Grange. The question was who was to suggest it. It would have come most easily from Cora, but Bruce was pretty sure that it would not occur to her to do so, nor would she prove amenable to any such offer on his part, either through herself or directly from him. It was to his grandfather he finally went.

'Grandpa, I have found out that Beverley has no plans for Christmas. There does not seem anybody to whom she could naturally go.'

'What's wrong with her staying here?'

133

'Nothing. Would you suggest it?'

'Of course. There's nothing I should like better. I'm going to miss that girl when she goes. I must confess she has managed to wriggle her way into my heart.'

Mine, too, thought Bruce, but he did not say it. 'You'll miss your chess, too, Grandpa. Still, it won't be yet. I should imagine it will be another six months before she gets to the end of it.'

'Yes, and then we shall have to think. Maybe we could offer her a job at the works if she would consider it.'

'That's a thought.' Bruce was glad the suggestion had come from his grandfather. 'Anyhow, we can leave that for the present. It is Christmas which is the trouble now.'

'You can leave that to me. I'll choose my time.' Cora's name had not been mentioned between them, but she had loomed large in both their thoughts.

John Sheavyn chose the time when they were all at the evening meal.

'What about Christmas, Beverley?' he asked. 'Have you got anything fixed up yet? If you haven't we should be very pleased if you would spend it here. Cora's brother is coming up. That's so, isn't it, Cora?' He turned to his grandson's wife.

'Yes.' Cora's answer was monosyllabic.

134

What was behind the old man's invitation? Cora could never believe in altruistic motives.

'So you see we shall be quite a party. Will you stay?'

'I should love to.' Beverley found her eyes straying in Bruce's direction. He had not spoken at all but she felt sure that the invitation had originated with him.

It was John Sheavyn, too, who mentioned the Boxing Day Meet. 'You might take Beverley along to see the Meet on Boxing Day at Ambleside,' he had said. 'I expect she might find it interesting.'

'So I might. Have you ever been to a meet, Beverley?' asked Bruce.

'No, but I can't ride.'

'That won't matter. I don't mean to say that you would not enjoy it much more if you could, but you can follow in your car and meet us at the strategic points. I should think that you will find it quite interesting. It will be a new experience.'

'You're welcome to it.' Cora shivered realistically. 'I loathe these hunts. Gilbert and I will keep the fire warm while you go to the hunt.'

Beverley wondered what Gilbert Marrow was like. Bruce had expressed no opinion whatever, and she did not feel she could ask him. One of the matters which she could not

135

discuss with Bruce was, naturally, his wife— or her relations.

Florence was not so reticent about the visitor-to-be. Beverley had purposely avoided any reference to him, being only too aware that Florence's verdict was hardly likely to be unbiased. It was very unlikely that she would look with favour on Cora Sheavyn's brother.

'I hear Prince Charming's coming for Christmas.' Florence handed the big wooden spoon over to Beverley. 'Here, have your stir and wish.'

'Who is Prince Charming?' Beverley was trying to do three things at once, to stir the heavy mass of the pudding mixture, to make the wish—what did she want most of all?—to discover who Prince Charming was.

'Her ladyship's brother.' What scorn Florence managed to infuse into that single word 'ladyship'.

'Oh, yes.' How slow she had been. Knowing that Gilbert Marrow was coming and noting the sarcasm behind Florence's statement, she ought to have been able to put two and two together and make the required four. 'Why Prince Charming? Is he very good-looking?'

'Very. He is a charming young man.' Such a pronouncement could only have come from Matthew.

136

'If you like them that way. Here, Matthew, you take the spoon.' She pushed the spoon into her husband's hand. 'He's good-looking, all right, but in my opinion he's a sissy. I like a man to be a man.'

'How old is he?' asked Beverley.

'About twenty-seven I should think. Oh, he's not so bad. It's a wonder he's as good as he is when you think how that woman worships him. I believe she practically brought him up. The mother died when he was tiny.'

Beverley found that she was looking forward with interest to meeting Gilbert Marrow. The fact that Bruce never spoke of him made it obvious to her that he did not like him much, but he could not be so bad if Florence was prepared to speak quite well of him. Christmas, she felt, promised to be quite exciting. She wondered whether it would be a white Christmas. This was just the place which called for a white Christmas, a real, old-fashioned Christmas.

Since she had passed her test she had spent many hours in learning the district. The shortness of the daylight hours, the often inclement weather, had restricted her activities, confined her explorations to the nearer lakes, but she was now thoroughly at home with these. Windermere, Grasmere, Rydal Water—she knew them all, but it was

Grasmere that she loved the most. She had left the car and wandered round the shores of the lake, up the fells. There were days when even the lower fells were draped in snow—in spite of the fact that, contrary to predictions, the weather was still comparatively mild. There were many more days when the upper slopes were wrapped in their white mantle. The only trees, apart from the evergreens, which still retained their leaves were the beeches—they still sported their golden-brown foliage. As Beverley climbed the hillsides she discovered that even now there were signs of the spring, the daffodils were shooting their green spikes through the black soil, telling of a golden glory to come. And there was the winter jasmine. In spite of the gales, the grey sky, the occasional snow, it trailed its golden flowers along the garden walls. Beverley loved it all as it was, but she loved it even more for the promise of what would be.

Those days in December were good days, happy days, days when she almost forgot that the ugly spectre of attempted murder had reared its ugly head but such a short time ago. Cora, too, seemed to have acquired a certain amount of peacefulness. If she did spit and snarl, Beverley saw no sign of it.

Maybe, thought the girl, Cora had just been going through an exceptionally bad time, perhaps she was not naturally quite so bad. It might even be that she had turned over a new leaf. Perhaps the knowledge of what she had nearly done had frightened her, shown her a side of herself which she had not known she possessed. Whatever the cause in that month before Christmas not a ripple disturbed the serenity of life at Willerton Grange.

CHAPTER EIGHT

'Beverley Gordon, my brother Gilbert.' Cora performed the introductions.

So this was Gilbert Marrow. Beverley had just entered the dining-room when the introduction was made. She had known that the young man had arrived several hours earlier, but this was her first sight of him. He was not at all as she had visualised him. Quite why she should have expected to find him to be a fair young man she could not have said, perhaps because of Florence's designation of 'sissy'. He had not even got his sister's tawny colouring. He was dark, very dark. His immaculately waved hair—it might have been fresh from the hairdresser's attentions—was blue-black in hue, his skin was a warm olive. He is beautiful, thought Beverley. No wonder Cora nearly worshipped him. He must have been an adorable little boy. As the evening progressed she discovered that his charm was not confined to his looks. He has got buckets of it, she thought.

Dinner that Christmas Eve was a much more sociable affair than normally. Cora, stimulated by her brother's company, really sparkled in a way that Beverley had never seen previously. She even deigned to laugh at John Sheavyn's tales, and John Sheavyn was in great form that evening, responsive to the unusually relaxed atmosphere. Why can't it be like this oftener? thought Bruce Sheavyn.

'Do you really have to go back on Tuesday?' Cora asked. It was obviously not the first time she had asked this question. They were in the library after dinner. During the holiday they were all the guests of John Sheavyn for the greater part of the day. Bruce had insisted that Christmas should be a family affair, a family of which Beverley was to be part. Cora had raised many objections, had wanted to restrict the celebrations to the three of them, to their own apartments, but her husband had been adamant.

'Yes, we shall be pleased to have you longer if you can stay, Gilbert.' Bruce added his invitation. For his own part, he would readily have dispensed with his brother-in-law's company altogether. They had little in common, but for Cora's sake he was willing not only to tolerate him, but even to make a show of welcoming him.

'I'm sure you could, Gilbert. Christmas is always a slack time for estate agents.' Cora knew that Christmas was a slack time for her brother's business and also that he was very far from being a king-pin in the concern. The business had originally belonged to her—she and her brother had been partners in it but Gilbert had been more or less a figurehead, he had merely lent a masculinity to the business. Cora had been the business woman. When she married she had sold her share in the firm to a man who was now the leading partner but had, as part of the agreement, had to accept Gilbert Marrow as an almost sleeping, but ever-present, partner.

'Sorry, Cora, but I promised to be back.' Gilbert still succeeded in hanging on to his belief that he was a valuable member of the firm. The fact that a third partner had entered the business had done nothing to undermine this.

'Have you an estate agency? Is it interesting?' Beverley, at one time had contemplated going into an estate agent's office. Gilbert, with his charm, ought to be excellent in such a business, she thought, not knowing that there was very little behind the charm.

'Quite, but I miss Cora. She knew how to make things hum. Why she ever got married, I don't know. Sorry, Bruce.' The young man gave a nervous laugh—he was never really at ease with his brother-in-law. 'I expect you know why.'

Do I? wondered Bruce. He looked round at

the members of this small family group assembled in the pleasant room. The library had returned to its accustomed neatness. The crates which had for so long disfigured it had gone, the new shelves had been put up, the books stood upon them in orderly array. On the hearth blazed a log fire, throwing out the scent of the burning apple tree branches. The four young people, the old man, sat round it in seeming amity, but Bruce Sheavyn knew that the amity was on the surface only. Cora looked at peace now, she was happy in her brother's company but that peace would be only transitory. He knew only too well that his wife bitterly resented his grandfather, that there were times when she barely tolerated himself. What had Cora hoped to get out of marriage? Whatever it had been she certainly had not got it. How much was he to blame? Would Cora have been happier if he had agreed to live in a small house in the suburbs? He very much doubted it. She would have had no more scope then, no more useful work for that over-active brain. He had thought latterly that it might have been good for Cora had she been able to take a job, but in the early days it had never entered his head. He had hoped that his wife would soon have the interest of motherhood. Now, he felt most strongly, that any such suggestion on his part would be received with contumely.

He was right in thinking that Cora would have welcomed a job, but it was not just any job that Cora Sheavyn wanted. She wanted a directorship, a leading part in the business of John Sheavyn and Son. It was this that she had hoped for when she married Bruce. Marriage as such had never appealed to her. She was a business woman at heart but she had wanted the status of a married woman. As the years had passed and she had reached her thirties without any sign of attaining the married state she had become afflicted with the fear that she never would get married. When she met Bruce Sheavyn she exerted every ounce of womanly charm which she could muster. In Bruce she thought she had found the answer to all her problems. He was young enough for her to influence, he was a partner in a family business where the only other partner was an ageing grandfather. These thoughts raced through Cora Sheavyn's mind as she waited for her husband's reply, a reply which did not come.

'Do you know why?' she asked him finally, voice and eyes alike exuding more than a touch of malice. There were still times when her good-natured mask slipped.

'I thought I did,' Bruce said quietly. 'Grandpa, do you think you would like to go in

144

the car with Beverley on Boxing Day, to follow the Meet?' He changed the subject deliberately. 'You don't think it would be too cold for you, do you?'

'Go, and catch your death of cold.' Cora could have shouted the words aloud. It was in her treatment of her husband's grandfather that she had made the mistake in the first days of her marriage. She had thought that an old man of seventy-three would have one foot in the grave, that on his grandson's recovery he would retire. Even when that had not happened, she had concluded that he would be merely a cipher in the business. She could not have been more wrong on all counts. Not only was John Sheavyn still very much alive, not only did he still retain an interest in the work, but he had a very definite poking finger in all its concerns. Had she only realised earlier that this was to be the case she would have acted differently, instead of ignoring him and alienating him she would have tried to behave as Beverley did now. Not that Beverley Gordon seemed to have any axe to grind, nevertheless she had certainly wormed her way into the old man's affections. Had she, Cora, behaved like Beverley, a directorship or something similar would be in her pocket by now, even though she was a woman, and she felt quite sure that John Sheavyn would not naturally be partial to a woman director. Not that it would have been easy for her to act in that manner. She was not the natural ray of sunshine that Beverley appeared to be but she could have done it—for the sake of what it would bring. As it was, she hated the old man, longed for his death, and there were times when she also hated Beverley Gordon, and for more reasons than because she had won the goodwill which would have been invaluable to her.

Beverley, the odd one in this company, was not unaware of the cross currents flowing between the others. She was conscious of the fact that they were in two camps, two hostile camps bound together by the uneasy relationship between Bruce and Cora. Bruce and his grandfather were united in ties of love, Cora and her brother were equally, if not more so, united in similar bonds. What was Gilbert really like? she wondered. He seemed charming enough but the point was how deep did the charm go? There was sometimes a queer glint in his eye when he looked at her. Why was Bruce so obviously lukewarm in his liking for him? Could it be rooted in jealousy, because Cora made no secret of the fact that her brother mattered far more to her than did her husband? She did not think that was so. Not only did jealousy seem so alien to Bruce's nature, but she much doubted if Bruce nowadays had enough love for his wife to engender that emotion. He might have had it in the early days though. That might account for his dislike of a man who, as far as she could judge on this short acquaintance appeared eminently likeable. Christmas Day was to bring a slight, though only slight revision of her appraisal of Gilbert Marrow.

'Will you come in the car to church, Beverley? We can walk back if you like.' Christmas Day had not brought the snow which Beverley had hoped for, but it was a sunny, crisp morning. She had intended to walk to church, but Bruce had waylaid her and suggested that she join them in the large car which would hold all five comfortably. She agreed readily, delighted that she would have Bruce's company on the homeward way.

'You two are fiends for walking,' Cora said as she opened the car door. 'Don't be late for Christmas dinner.'

'No fear.' Bruce closed the door on her. He and Beverley stood for a moment watching the retreating car. Suddenly Beverley was filled with an unreasoning fear. Cora had got Mr. Sheavyn in that car with no Bruce at hand to keep a check on her. What might happen? Would Cora make another attempt on his life? For weeks this fear had lain in abeyance, been lulled to sleep by the span of uneventful, peaceful days. Now it sprang into being once more. She half-turned to Bruce, to tell him to stop the car, but it was too late. Even if it had not been, she realised she could not have asked him. She could have given no reasonable explanation. Anyhow, she told herself, she was being silly. Gilbert was in the car with them. Even if Cora had any evil intentions she would not do anything with a third person present, not, at least, when that third person was her beloved brother.

'It's a glorious morning for walking.' Bruce's voice shook her out of her fears.

'Yes, but we haven't got Matthew's snow for Christmas.' Matthew was one of those old countrymen who was possessed of a weather wisdom. Bruce, who had had occasion to go to Carlisle the previous week had reported seeing whooper swans and ducks on the lakes.

'That means we are in for a cold spell,' Matthew had said. 'We'll be having a white Christmas yet.'

'No,' said Bruce now, 'but it's definitely colder. He was right in that.'

Much though she enjoyed that walk with Bruce, Beverley found that, for once, she was glad when they reached home. Try as she would she could not quite banish the niggling doubt that she ought not to have agreed to that walk, that she ought to have thought of the possible danger to Mr. Sheavyn. She made straight for the kitchen when she had left Bruce.

'Everything all right, Florence?' she asked. Had anything happened, the kitchen staff would be the first people to hear.

'Yes, Miss Beverley. Did you think I'd burnt the turkey?' Florence was at the stove, stirring something in a pan.

'It smells good.' Beverley sniffed appreciatively. Her mind was at rest now.

'It is good.' Florence had no false modesty about her cooking. 'As you'll find out in a few minutes. Now, off you go, Miss Beverley, I can't abide anyone round when I'm doing all these last-minute jobs.'

'Sorry, Florence. I'm gone.' Beverley suited the action to the words.

Florence's dinner proved as good as she had promised. It was a pleasant meal, gracious, dignified. Beverley could not help contrasting it with her last Christmas dinner. In spite of the fact that tensions had eased, that each member of the party had most obviously made a determined effort to shelve all differences, there was not that Christmas spirit that had been such a marked feature of the previous Christmas. The difference was not, Beverley felt, due only to the unlikeness of the setting, to the contrast between the near formality of this meal and the noisy freedom of the other. Sandra's eldest brother had been there with his family, three small children. Was it the presence of the children which made that intrinsic difference? Was it because there had been children there, that last Christmas had been the most truly festive one she had ever known?

'Were there any children at your friend's last Christmas, Beverley?' Bruce might have read her thoughts.

'Yes. The eldest son came back with his three children.'

'Is that the friend who has just become engaged?' Cora had accepted the fact that Beverley's expected arrangements had fallen through but, until now had evinced no further interest.

'Yes.'

'Have you met the fiancé, and do you approve?'

'Yes, I have, and do,' smiled Beverley. She realised that Cora's questions stemmed more from a desire to keep the ball of conversation rolling than genuine interest, but she hoped she would not flog the subject too much. Too many enquiries into her past could only result in boredom for everyone.

'What is he like?'

'Quite nice-looking.' The tone was laconic, intended to squash further questions, but it did not achieve its object.

'What is his name?' Gilbert had joined the chase. Out of pure devilment, she felt certain.

'And when are they going to be married?' It had become a game now. Beverley was grateful for this last question. It gave her a chance to checkmate.

'When they have got some money. And that's the end of Solomon Grundy.' She turned to Bruce. 'Does Cora's Christmas flower arrangement meet with your approval?' she asked.

'Neatly turned.' Bruce laughed. 'But you knew the answer to that one before you asked it.'

'Yes,' smiled Beverley. It would be impossible to imagine that anyone could disapprove of the centrepiece which added the final touch to an already attractive array. The white of the Christmas roses blended with the green leaves and the red berries of the holly with an artistry which showed it to be the work of a master hand.

The rest of the day passed pleasantly. There were no untoward scenes, no acrimonious words, no backbiting innuendoes to mar the spirit of seeming goodwill. The only trouble as far as Beverley was concerned was Gilbert

Marrow's attitude to her. She doubted whether any of the others would be aware that there could be anything amiss, so nearly imperceptible were those sidelong glances which he shot at her from time to time, but she knew them for what they were. During the last two years she had encountered too often the questing stares of the opposite sex not to be able to recognise them. She was thankful that they were such a close-knit party, that Cora was so leech-like where her brother was concerned.

The next day Beverley woke up to a world wrapped in white. Matthew's white Christmas had come a day too late, but it was none the less beautiful for that. Would it make any difference to the Hunt? Beverley had not the slightest idea whether hunts were affected by the weather or not. After breakfast she went in search of Bruce to discover whether the assignment still held.

'Yes, they are sure to hold it but the weather is far from ideal for it. It will be still less ideal for you as a watcher, so I suggest we go along to see the huntsmen and the hounds assemble in the Market Place at Ambleside and then go off on our own. I can go tomorrow if it is fit. You insist on working then so we might as well do something else today.' Since Christmas Day fell on a Sunday, Tuesday had been declared to be an extra Bank Holiday. Consequently Bruce would be at home, but Beverley had been adamant in her decision that she did not need an extra day.

'Are you certain you don't want to go both days?' she asked now.

'Quite certain. Meet me at the front door in a quarter of an hour and we will go to Ambleside.'

It was the first time Beverley had witnessed a meet. She was entranced by the scene in the Market Square. The red coats of the huntsmen were even more colourful than usual when seen in relief against the whiteness of the snow. The square was packed, not only with the members of the hunt, but also with sightseers.

'There is always a big crowd on Boxing Day,' explained Bruce. They stood there until the last of the red-coated men, the last of the hounds had disappeared. 'What about going over to Derwentwater?' asked Bruce. 'We are not expected back to lunch. It should be more beautiful than ever today.'

They went to Derwentwater, to Bassenthwaite, hesitated as to whether they should go over the Honister Pass to Buttermere, but decided against it.

'It might be a bit tricky today,' Bruce decided. 'Anyhow, you have had quite an eyeful today.'

'It's been perfect.' Beverley was almost glad that Bruce had decided against Honister, not because she was nervous but because she felt that she had seen as much beauty as she could absorb in one day. She was unusually silent during the drive back.

'Are you tired?' asked Bruce, unable to account for this withdrawn mood.

'No, just satiated with beauty.'

'Yes, it is rather breathtaking,' agreed Bruce. 'I hope you won't be too satiated to take tea with us this afternoon,' he laughed.

'Oh, no, it's not that sort of satiation.' Beverley leaned back in the seat, content-filled.

'We might as well leave our coats in the cloakroom,' suggested Bruce when they reached the house. 'There is no need for you to go up to your own rooms.' He led the way into the cloakroom which led off the hall. At the door of his own apartment he stopped. 'You go in,' he said, putting his key in the door. 'I'll go and see if Grandpa is ready.' He left Beverley to announce herself.

'You'll manage it. Anybody you want to get rid of, you will. You are clever enough for that.'

The sitting-room door had opened before Beverley had had time to knock, and Gilbert

Marrow came out, throwing the words over his shoulder, into the room behind him. Beverley wondered which of them looked the most taken aback. Certainly Gilbert's mouth had dropped open and she felt pretty sure that her own was in no better state. Gilbert was the first to recover.

'Hello, Beverley.' He pulled the door to behind him, his voice little more than a whisper. 'Where have you dropped from?'

'Bruce had just let me in. He has gone for his grandfather.'

'And now you are wondering who my sister wants to get rid of? Well, let me tell you at once, it isn't you. It isn't a case of listeners hearing no good of themselves.' Beverley did not feel at all convinced of the truth of his next words. 'I had better tell you what it was all about otherwise you might not believe me. There's a fellow in Ambleside who has been pestering Cora. She was wondering whether she ought to tell Bruce, but I tell her that she is perfectly capable of chalking off the fellow herself. But don't let her know I told you. She would be furious with me if she knew I had told you, but what else could I do? You would never have believed me otherwise, would you?'

'No,' agreed Beverley. She did not add that she was equally sceptical of the truth of this story.

'You knock at the door and I will let you in,' he said. Long before this he had pushed her through the further door and carried on the conversation in the corridor, still in the hushed tones which he had adopted from the outset. 'We mustn't let Cora have any idea that you heard anything.' Beverley did as he requested, allowed herself to be received by him. He opened the sitting-room door. 'Here's Beverley,' he called to Cora. 'Bruce has gone for his grandfather.'

Beverley tried to behave as though nothing untoward had occurred, but throughout that period in Cora's room, and for the rest of the day, she was acutely disturbed, trying to account not only for Cora's words, but also for her brother's subsequent explanation of them. Why had he troubled to weave such an obviously false tale, or did he not realise how phoney it sounded? Who was it that Cora could get rid of if she wanted to? She might be wrong but she thought she could narrow the contestants for that place down to two, herself or Mr. Sheavyn. She rather fancied it was herself this time. Why, otherwise, should Gilbert have been at such pains to tell her that it was not? And what had Cora told Gilbert?

She was more than thankful when that evening came to an end. The holiday to which she had looked forward so much had gone sour on her. It was not only the afternoon's episode which worried her. The cloak of goodwill under which her companions had tried to hide their differences was wearing thin. They had been in too close proximity for too long. It would be good to get away from them all tomorrow, to get on with her work. Above all it would be good to get away from Gilbert Marrow. She did not trust him in any way. His charm had lost all its power as far as she was concerned. Probably, she admitted, because she now knew him to be of the type she so disliked.

She did not know that it was to Cora she owed her immunity from Gilbert's attentions, but Cora had no intention of allowing her young brother to become entangled with so unimportant a person as Beverley. When Gilbert did marry, he had so far shown no signs of wishing to do so, it must be to somebody of both wealth and importance. Not only did Cora realise that her brother would never be wealthy from his own efforts, but she felt that his charm was such that he was worthy to shine with the highest—or at least to be a star in a much higher sky than he had been born to. When she knew that Beverley was to be at Willerton Grange for Christmas she had determined that Gilbert should have no opportunity of being alone with the girl and so far she had succeeded. It was for this reason that she had raised no objection to her husband taking the girl to the Boxing Day Meet. Better Bruce than Gilbert, she had thought, confident that she had already scotched the possibilities of danger in that direction.

It was not until he was on the point of departure that Gilbert had even a few minutes alone with Beverley, and then Beverley was fore-armed. As she had said good night the previous evening he had said:

'I'll see you before I go, Beverley. You'll be in the library tomorrow morning, won't you?' The words had been innocent enough, but the accompanying smile was far from guileless. Beverley determined that the farewell would be far more formal than Gilbert Marrow intended. Her first task the following morning on entering the library had been to draw her desk across one corner of the room. When Gilbert entered she was firmly ensconced behind it, her typewriter yet another barrier between her and any unwelcome attentions.

'Heavens above, Beverley!' he exclaimed as she rose and held out a hand to him. 'Do you always entrench yourself in like this when you work. Come on, girl, come on out of your fortifications and say goodbye to a fellow properly.' He began to push the desk aside, but Cora's voice halted him.

'Gilbert! It's time we were going.'

'Blast! Oh, well, we'll do better at Easter.'

'Gilbert!' It was a clarion call this time.

'Coming!' He turned to join his sister, but was back before he had reached the door. He took Beverley's hand in his. 'Goodbye,' he said. 'We will manage to see more of each other next time. Easter isn't such a closed-shop affair as Christmas. We'll ...' Cora's angry face appeared at the door.

'*Are* you coming, Gilbert?' She flashed Beverley an irate glance.

'Yes,' but before he followed his sister he turned for a last word. 'Thumbs up for Easter,' he mouthed, suiting the action to the words.

Beverley, watching his retreating back, struggled with conflicting emotions. There was relief that he had gone, annoyance at his assumption that his maleness was all-conquering, but there was also amusement. He was so ingenuous, so childishly confident, so completely blind to the lack of reciprocity evinced by Beverley herself. She shrugged her shoulders.

'You won't be seeing me at Easter, Mr. Gilbert Marrow,' she said to the empty room. 'Not if I know anything about it.'

CHAPTER NINE

The aftermath of Christmas was felt by all the members of the household in varying degrees. For Bruce Sheavyn those days after Christmas were the beginning of an inward torment which, he felt, must be with him till the end of his days. He had long realised that his love for his wife had gradually dwindled until it was little more than toleration, but as long as it was toleration, so long was life correspondingly tolerable, but at some time during these last days that toleration had vanished. He could not say at what particular point this had happened, but the realisation had come to him at some time between Christmas Eve and the departure of his brother-in-law that not only did he not love his wife, but that his feelings for her approximated to hatred. He told himself that this feeling must have been building up for months, but it was only now that it had struck him with the ferocity of a hurricane, and the knowledge had shocked him to the core.

'Aren't you well, Bruce?' John Sheavyn had not been slow to notice his grandson's depression. He did not associate it with Cora. In the past he had often wondered how the

160

young man could retain his natural cheerfulness when married to a woman like Cora, but he had come to accept the fact that however disillusioned Bruce might be with his wife—and he had no doubt that there had been disillusionment—he had evolved a philosophy which enabled him to face up to the situation not only with fortitude, but with a certain measure of happiness. 'Is the leg playing you up?' he asked.

'No, Grandpa. I'm all right.'

'Is there something amiss at the works?' persisted the old man.

'No, Grandpa,' he said once more.

'Well, there's something wrong, but obviously it's nothing in which I can help.' John Sheavyn knew his grandson well enough to recognise the fact that whatever the cause of the trouble Bruce was not prepared to share it.

'I'm sorry. Watch out for your bishop.' The conversation had taken place during one of their infrequent chess sessions. Bruce deliberately turned his grandfather's thoughts in another direction. Much though he would have liked to discuss his troubles with someone he was well aware that his grandfather was the last person in whom he should confide. The old man had never had any use for Cora.

The urge to confide in somebody had been

overwhelming. It could not be his grandfather. Who then could it be? He had no friend close enough for such a confidence. Cora, in the early days, had purposefully and successfully mutilated or destroyed his former friendships. Even as these thoughts passed through his mind he realised that, had those friendships still existed he would never have been able to bare his innermost thoughts to any one of his old friends.

Yet the need to do so was urgent. There were times when he was terrified as to where this repressed hate might lead him. He had to hide it, not only from Cora, but from the other members of his household. His sense of guilt made him for a time diligently attentive to his wife. Hitherto he had allotted Cora her fair share of guilt for the lack of success in their marriage; now he took it all unto himself. For the first time in his life he regretted that he was not a member of the Roman Catholic Church. Then he might have the relief of Confession. He could tell his trouble in the anonymity of the confessional box. But he was not a Roman Catholic, nor would he ever be able to accept the teaching of that church. He had got to fight this through for himself, by some means or other he had got to come out of this pit into the light of sanity. If only he could isolate some act, some word which had put the spark to this conflagration he would have a vantage point from which to fight, but he could not.

Cora, too, found herself ill at ease and more than usually frustrated during those weeks following Christmas. She missed Gilbert, but in her present frame of mind that was one of her minor worries. She had come to think that for once she had overrated her powers. Even before Christmas she had doubts as to whether her indoctrination of Beverley had been completely successful, but had jibbed at giving those doubts houseroom. On Boxing Day they had gatecrashed into her consciousness, refusing further denial. There had been a difference in the girl that evening. Cora had recognised it for what it was. She was not only in love, but she was aware of it. It was not necessary to note the direction of her glances to know the object of that love. It could only be Bruce, Cora's husband. As far as Cora could see, Bruce had shown no signs of being similarly afflicted. Cora was well aware that Bruce was fond of Beverley, but did not think that at present his feelings went beyond fondness, but she was awake to the fact that the girl's love was more than likely to act as tinder to transform that fondness into a living flame.

It was not often that Cora Sheavyn was nonplussed, but she was now. Gilbert had told her that she was clever enough to remove anyone from her path if she so desired, but she doubted her ability in this case. Both Bruce and his grandfather were too enamoured of this girl to agree to her leaving before the library was finished and Cora was quite sure that no argument of hers would have any effect. For the moment all she could do was to wait and see, and such a laissez-faire state of affairs was not good for Cora's temper even had it not been already frayed by worry about her brother. She was troubled about the relations between Gilbert and the new partner.

'Bruce,' she tackled her husband after a day which had been packed with minor annoyances, a day when a grey drizzle had added its quota to the general unsatisfactoriness of life. 'Couldn't Gilbert come and live here? There's plenty of room. As a matter of fact he could have Beverley's apartments when she goes. Surely that can't be long now. I can't think how she manages to stretch out the job for so long.'

'Beverley is not going.' Bruce spoke shortly, not troubling to raise his eyes from his hands. He was undoing his shoe-laces and he continued to do this. He took his slippers from the box, put them on, leaned back in his chair, studiously avoiding his wife's eyes. He was in

164

no mood for an argument. He had just returned from Kendal after a day when he had worked himself beyond any normal limit. Every day now was like this. He tried to drown his troubles in work, to make himself so unutterably weary that, when the day was over he had not the wherewithal to worry.

'Beverley is not going! What do you mean?' Cora was not going to let this pass.

'I mean that Beverley is going to stay on when she has finished the library. She is going into the firm.' His grandfather had already made the suggestion to Beverley and the girl had agreed with alacrity.

'Going into the firm!' Cora's voice had risen to a screech. 'And what is she going to do in the firm?'

'For the time being she is going into my office. What happens after depends on circumstances.' Bruce forced himself to speak quietly, to ignore the stridency of his wife's questions. 'If she would like and shows promise, she might become a buyer, but that is all in the air at present.' Bruce could not think why he was telling Cora all this. Why had he not been content to tell Cora merely that Beverley was to be in his office?'

'A buyer!' Cora laughed shrilly. 'That girl has played her cards well. To think an upstart like that can come in and be a buyer and your own wife has never been offered anything.'

'I only mentioned the possibility of a buyer.' Bruce cursed himself for his loquacity. 'I had no idea that you had ever wanted such a thing.' He spoke in all sincerity, but now the idea had been planted he knew that Cora's words were no idle ones, that she would have indeed liked to have been a member of the firm. He remembered how great a part she had played in business before her marriage; he was, at this late date, aware of her frustrations. Nevertheless, he could not but be thankful that she had not been invited to come into the firm, that realisation of its possibility had only just come to him. With Cora at the works he would have had no refuge.

'And Beverley Gordon is not only to be at Sheavyn's works, she is also to live at Sheavyn's home. Is that what you mean?'

'It is.'

'And I was never consulted,' stormed the woman.

'It was hardly necessary.' Guiltily Bruce realised that had relations between him and his wife been what they should have been, he might not have consulted her but he certainly would have told her. He tried to justify himself not only to Cora but to himself. 'After all both the firm and Willerton Grange are my grandfather's.'

'But it was your idea that Beverley Gordon should go into the firm and that she should remain here,' she accused him.

'No,' he denied. 'The idea was my grandfather's, but I can't see why it should concern you so much. The fact that she will work at Sheavyn's will not affect you and she is not going to live in our part of the house. You will not need to see much of her. But I thought you liked her.'

'Oh, so-so.' Cora decided she had better play her cards more carefully if she were to get her wish as far as Gilbert was concerned. 'But even if Beverley is staying here, there is plenty of room for Gilbert as well. He could get a job here.' She did not suggest that he also went to Sheavyn's. That might come later.

'Y-yes,' Bruce temporised. For a second he was tempted to agree. If Gilbert were here he would be relieved from much of his dancing attendance on Cora; he would, in fact, be very nearly superfluous as far as his wife was concerned. He would be breadwinner and not much else, a state of affairs which, in his present frame of mind, would suit him very well. Saner thoughts prevailed. If Gilbert Marrow once established himself at Willerton Grange, he would be there for ever, a source of irritation not only to Bruce himself, but also to his grandfather. The thought of his

167

grandfather made him realise that the decision would not be his alone. If Gilbert came, he would have to live in the main building, in his grandfather's home. 'No, Cora,' he spoke firmly, 'it would not work.' He could have hidden behind his grandfather, but he refused to do so. 'No,' as she opened her lips in protest. 'I am sorry, but I refuse to contemplate it.' He purposely refused to embroider his refusal knowing that any explanation he might offer would only add fuel to his wife's arguments.

'No, of course not,' she spat the words at him. She recognised the futility of further argument, but the recognition made her all the more bitter. 'There is room for your beloved Beverley, but none for my brother.' She flung out of the room, banging the door behind her.

'Your beloved Beverley!' It was true. He did love Beverley, but the words had had to be thrown at him before he knew it himself—and by his wife! Was it so obvious to others, or had it just been a shot in the dark on Cora's part? Was it because of that love, even though unrecognised, that his relations with Cora had worsened so rapidly? Had he suddenly seen what joy could lie in personal relationships, and consequently resented the travesty of his with Cora? He had not thought Cora to be jealous, but she might well be and that jealousy could have served to drive a wedge between them, driven them still further apart. Whatever Cora's feelings had been there was no doubt about them now. They went beyond the bounds of jealousy. There had been unconcealed hatred in her eyes when she spat Beverley's name at him. A shiver passed through him. Cora was not the type of person to let any passion lie dormant. She had been jealous of his friends in the past. Those friends had been liquidated as far as he was concerned. How much more would she strive to oust Beverley from his life, and with reason this time.

Beverley, herself, had her own troubles. They seemed to her to be manifold. Greatest of all was the knowledge which had hit her after Christmas, the knowledge that she was in love with Bruce Sheavyn. She had thought herself immune from that malady. The fact that she had played with the idea of the poor girl marrying the rich employer meant nothing. It had been mere fantasy. This was real. She was in love with this rich employer, but there the fairy tale finished. The rich employer was married and Beverley had heard too much obloquy from her mother on the subject of women who broke up marriages to reconcile herself to that role even though she knew Bruce's marriage to be far from ideal.

I shall just have to watch myself very carefully until Whitsuntide, she thought—she expected to finish the library by then—and then I must think up some excuse for not going to Sheavyn's.

In her ignorance, Beverley thought that the question of her love for Bruce was one which would yield with comparative ease to a display of firmness on her own part. From schooldays she dug up the quotation to the effect that she was master of her soul—or was it her fate? Whatever it was, surely a woman with sufficient strength of character should be able to keep her emotions in check. The fact that those two days at Christmas had left her with two other problems added colour to this supposition. Her love for Bruce had to share its position in her musings with those other two dilemmas. Gilbert's words, words which had never been intended for her ears, recurred to her time and time again. She could never finally make up her mind as to whom they had referred. Had it been she, herself, who was the object of Cora's ill-will? Was it she who was to be got rid of, to be dismissed, or, more sinisterly, was it John Sheavyn? As the weeks passed and Cora took no trouble to hide her hostility she decided that it was most probably she who was to be the victim, that Gilbert's over-assiduous protestations had been the poor cloak for the truth which she had originally thought them. Nevertheless she did not hide from herself the fact that John Sheavyn might still stand in grievous danger.

'Didn't you say that there were some books on yachting in the library?' asked Bruce one evening. He could have put the question some other time, at one of those sessions which he still occasionally spent with Beverley in the library, but conversation at dinner these days was so laboured that he welcomed any topic. Cora had responded to his refusal to give her brother harbourage by virtually sending him to Coventry. She spoke to him only when it was absolutely necessary. The ban on normal everyday communication made the times when they were thrown not only into each other's company, but also that of others, occasions of embarrassment and uneasiness. Hence Bruce's search for any undebatable topic. If Cora did trouble to speak it would be to question, to seek a quarrel. 'Do you think you could put your finger on them?'

Cora did not give Beverley time to reply. 'I shouldn't think Beverley could need more than a second to put her finger on any book in that library,' she said. 'Judging by the time she's been on the job she should know the position of every single book; its contents too, I should think,' she added.

171

'Don't talk rot, Cora.' Bruce Sheavyn spoke sharply.

'Naturally, I was not speaking literally, but you must admit that she has been an unconscionably long time on the job.' She looked across at Beverley, noting with pleasure her heightened colour. 'Of course I don't blame you for stretching it out,' her voice dripped with a honeyed malice. 'You'd go a long way to find a more comfortable job, wouldn't you? Isn't the proper word "sinecure"?'

'I'm not ...' Beverley found to her annoyance that her eyes were filling. She blinked rapidly. She ought to be used to such provocation by this time, to be used to Cora's unpleasant innuendoes. Since Christmas she had made no attempt to be pleasant to the girl, but had treated her with a cold contempt, ignoring her presence as far as possible. When she did speak to her it had been to make some carping criticism, but she had never before made those criticisms quite so public, quite so blatant. 'I am not making the job spin out.' Against her better judgment, Beverley was stung to take up her tormentor's challenge.

'Don't trouble to answer, Beverley.' Bruce took up the cudgels on her behalf. 'Cora may not know much about librarianship, but she knows enough to know that you are not "spinning it out". She is merely needling you. Cora,' he turned to his wife angrily. 'I think . . .'

'Will you serve the bird, sir, or shall I give it to the master?' Matthew stood by the young man's side, the heavy dish poised in his hands.

'I'll carve, Matthew.' The angry words were deflected, lost, but this was only one of the occasions when the old servant had witnessed some similar, if not quite so explosive, scene. Florence and Matthew were only too well aware of the uneasy relationship which existed between those whom they served. There were many times when they wondered what would be the upshot, whether they too would be caught up in the threatened maelstrom.

'They've been at it again,' he said to his wife that evening. 'If I were Mr. Bruce I'd take a stick to that woman.'

'She'd get her own back somehow.' Florence doubted the efficacy of such methods.

'Aye, and she's getting her own back on Miss Beverley for something or other.' He described the scene in the dining-room.

'I hear as her ladyship's got her knife into you now,' Florence greeted Beverley the next morning when she made her usual eleven o'clock appearance in the kitchen.

'Oh, did Matthew tell you?' Beverley felt

uneasy these days when Florence inveighed against Cora. Though she might agree with every word that was said the participation in the conversation gave her a feeling of guilt. The knowledge that she was in love with Cora's husband—however innocent and hidden that love might be—endowed the woman with a strange immunity from her own criticism. She believed that she owed a certain loyalty to the woman, however misplaced that loyalty, just as she felt that in loving Cora's husband she was doing her a wrong. She could not rid herself of these convictions however many times she assured herself that, since nobody would ever know, her love could harm nobody.

'I think she was just feeling wrong side out,' she tried to brush the incident away.

'From what I hear she always is wrong side out these days. Did you know Mrs. Groves is leaving?' Mrs. Groves was the 'marvellous' cook of whom Cora had spoken on Beverley's first day at Willerton Grange. 'She's lasted longer than any other of Mrs. Bruce's staff, but she's come to the end of her tether. Says she can do nothing right these days.'

Mrs. Groves' defection was a straw in the wind, an outward sign of the unhappy conditions which prevailed in the left wing of the house. For his own part the present state of affairs suited Bruce. He found this state of armed neutrality infinitely easier to bear than the previous no-man's-land of uneasy truce. The knowledge that he loved Beverley had not yet made its full impact. Ostrich-like he shut his mind to the probable consequences. Having found the reason for his feelings towards his wife, he had also found the means of exorcising them. He no longer hankered after the catharsis of confession. He had come to terms with himself. He had no delusions as to the probable temporary nature of this relief, but for the present he was content to let things ride.

Those months of winter seemed to Beverley to stretch into eternity. Even her work had begun to pall. The constant cataloguing had become monotonous. She probably would not have noticed it so much had the atmosphere in the house been different. It was only when she was in John Sheavyn's study, when she was playing chess that she could escape from these tensions. She saw so little of Bruce that she wondered if she had offended him in some way. She was not to know of Cora's words, words which labelled her as Bruce's beloved. The words had left their sting, engendered a certain wariness by their very truth.

Beverley's greatest joy was the car. If she owed nothing else to Cora, she did owe her this. It was at Cora's instigation that she had learned to drive, it was her help which had started her on the path. Now there were few days when she did not go far afield, driving herself to some remote spot where she could leave the car and wander through the countryside. It was all so new and fresh to her. She had never been at such close quarters with nature, certainly had never been in the country at this time of the year, and in spite of early Jonahs, the winter had proved unusually mild. There had been days in January when one might have suspected that spring was on the way. As the days progressed, she looked for, and discovered, the first signs of spring. She found her first snowdrops, she saw her first new-born lamb. Much she discovered for herself. Very occasionally it was the country-born Bruce who introduced her to the wonders of a northern spring.

Those days of the early part of the year went very slowly. The cataloguing of the library seemed an almost endless task. Most of the books had found their own special niches on the shelves but there was still the monumental work of indexing them. There was no longer the same escape into the everyday life of the household. There was nothing but tension. Cora no longer sought Beverley's company, even Bruce sought it very little. Only John

Sheavyn's attitude to her was unchanged. Beverley began to count the weeks to Easter—which she was going to spend with Sandra in London. There, at least, she would be away from all these cross currents which bore her thoughts hither and thither, giving them no resting place.

CHAPTER TEN

'I think I shall go into the works tomorrow, Bruce.' It was weeks since John Sheavyn had paid a visit to his works. The winter, though it had not been severe, had proved trying to him and he had been content to potter about at home. Content was perhaps hardly the word, he had chafed at his inactivity, but had realised the necessity. The signs of the near approach of spring, the thrusting green spikes in the garden, had given him a new life and with it the desire to renew his personal contacts with his business—he had maintained a lively interest in it throughout these months at home, but that was only second-hand. He wanted to see for himself.

'Good, Grandpa. Will it be too early for you to go in with me? Or would you rather get Matthew to run you in?'

'I could...' began Beverley, but John Sheavyn was before her.

'No, it won't be too early. I will go in with you and I'll get a bus back. There's no need to trouble Matthew.'

'I can run you back if you like. I have got to go to Kendal tomorrow.'

It would be difficult to say which one of the

remaining trio at the table was the most surprised at Cora's offer. John Sheavyn had never known her to make any such suggestion before. Nevertheless, he was more than ready to accept what looked like a peace offering.

'Thank you, Cora. That would be very good of you if it is not going to inconvenience you in any way.'

'No, Mr. Sheavyn, I can suit my time to yours.'

Both Beverley and Bruce looked at Cora in amazement. Such amenability was out of character where Cora was concerned at the best of times. In the light of her recent behaviour it was breathtaking. Beverley had a sudden clutch of fear. Was this part of some plot on Cora's part? Was she once more going to make an attempt on Mr. Sheavyn's life? She wanted to say something, to suggest that she should bring the old man back from Kendal, but what reason could she give for such a suggestion? Cora had said it would cause her no inconvenience. How then could she suggest that she, Beverley, should make a special journey into Kendal for the purpose?

'You are sure it is no trouble, Cora?' Bruce, too, was at a loss to account for this change of front. Not that it was so very sudden. There had been a gradual softening in Cora's behaviour over the last week. Ever since Mrs.

Groves had given in her notice. Had that given her a jolt? Had it made her realise how her ill temper could only react on herself? It must be most unpleasant to be at odds with every other member of the household, and that had been Cora's state since Christmas.

It was not the discomfort of her present situation which had prompted Cora's change of mind. It was the thought of the future. She had not given up the hope that John Sheavyn's days were numbered; either by nature on its own or by nature given a helping hand by Cora Sheavyn, she did not yet know. If nature did not come up to scratch she had every intention of lending that helping hand, or even doing the whole job herself if the opportunity occurred. And when John Sheavyn did die, it would be as well if she were on fairly good terms with her husband. She had also decided very definitely that Beverley Gordon had to go, but not yet. She might—it was only a possibility but it was one—prove a whipping boy if and when that desired something did happen to the owner of Willerton Grange. In the meantime she must walk carefully, she must try to sow seeds of distrust of Beverley Gordon in her husband's mind. So far, as she had expected, those seeds had fallen on stony ground: they were even threatening to spring up into weeds which might strangle the sower.

But there had been one seed, sown unawares, which might yet bear fruit. The words 'your beloved Beverley' had come on the spur of the moment. They had had no ulterior motive, but Cora had a shrewd suspicion that they had hit their mark. Bruce had been seeing less of Beverley Gordon lately.

The next morning, Beverley found it impossible to keep her mind on her work. The figure of John Sheavyn would persist in obtruding itself between herself and her indexing. Sometimes it would be accompanied by that of Cora, Cora with an evil smile on her face, a smile of malignant triumph. As the time drew near for Cora's return she became more and more restless. Cora had agreed to pick Mr. Sheavyn up at twelve o'clock. It had been a sunny morning when they had left, but now the sky was heavily cloudladen, a strong wind shook the trees, chased the clouds across the background greyness. The minutes passed. There had been more than time for the journey yet there was still no sign of the car— Beverley had taken her work to the window where she had a view of the drive, would be able to glimpse its first appearance.

As the time passed and there was still no car she became more and more anxious, more and more self-recriminatory. She ought never to have let this happen. By some means or other—she could not even now think what—she ought to have put a stop to this drive. Matthew came in with her lunch.

'Will you put my tray here, Matthew?' she asked.

'Are you sure you would not like it near the fire, Miss Beverley?' Matthew looked at her in surprise. 'It's not much of a day to sit near the window today.'

'No, thank you, Matthew, I would rather have it here.' She almost told him of her fears but stopped in time. Matthew could do nothing if those fears had any justification and if they had not, if the delay proved to be due to normal happenings—and she kept on telling herself that this could easily be the case—she would certainly regret having voiced her suspicions.

'The master's late back. He should have been in for lunch.' Matthew's words cut across her own anxieties.

'I expect something cropped up at the last minute.' She had tried to comfort herself with that theory.

'Maybe. I hope you're right, but I don't like it. It's not like Mr. Sheavyn to be late.'

They had still not returned when Matthew came back for her tray. He stationed himself by the window. 'I wish they'd come,' he muttered.

'They're here!' Beverley's quick eyes saw the nose of the big car appearing round a bend. Her first reaction was one of relief, but it was immediately superseded by apprehension. The car was there, but what might it contain? The presence of the car did not mean that all was well with John Sheavyn. She could hardly restrain herself from rushing out to meet the approaching vehicle. Common sense prevailed yet again. If John Sheavyn was safe and well, her conduct would look not only silly—it might appear suspicious to Cora, and to arouse Cora's suspicions might increase Mr. Sheavyn's danger—if it did exist. She did sometimes wonder if she had not imagined that last episode, or if she had not imagined it if she had misinterpreted it.

'He's all right,' she breathed. Cora had got out of the car, and gone round to the door and helped the old gentleman out.

'Aye, thank God.' Matthew looked at her queerly. Had he suspected her unease? wondered Beverley. 'She's mighty solicitous all of a sudden,' muttered the old man.

Cora was indeed shepherding her husband's father with an air of unusual attention. Matthew went to open the front door. Beverley still stood and watched. A gust of wind tugged at the scarf wound round Cora's head. She must have been to the hairdresser's; those were the only occasions on which Cora wore a head-scarf. Beverley realised how the weather had changed since early morning. Then the sun had been shining; the trees scarcely moved. Now the sky was overcast; the branches struggled in the grip of a vicious wind. Beverley shuddered as she turned away—Mr. Sheavyn and Cora had disappeared from her view—and went back to her neglected lunch.

'Sorry we are late, Matthew.' The words reached her through the partly open door. Matthew had left it ajar. Had he done it on purpose, so that she would know that all was well with his master? The sound of John Sheavyn's voice put her mind at ease. Her fears had been ungrounded. Once more she had misjudged Cora. 'There was a slight hitch in our arrangements,' Mr. Sheavyn went on to explain.

It was not until the evening that she learned about that slight hitch. What she did learn then made her feel that Cora had not been completely blameless, though in view of the explanation she felt that even her suspicious nature—and she had come to the conclusion that she must have a very suspicious nature as far as Cora was concerned—could not pin any evil intention on to the woman.

'Has your grandfather told you what happened this morning?' she asked her husband as they sat down to dinner.

'What happened? What do you mean?' Bruce looked at his wife sharply. 'Since this is the first time I have seen Grandfather since he left the works he can hardly have told me anything. What did happen?' He was at a loss to know whether the happening was good or ill.

'It was nothing.' John Sheavyn tried to push the matter aside. 'It was nobody's fault.'

'Fault?' Bruce was alerted. 'What did happen?' he asked again.

'I should have picked Mr. Sheavyn up at twelve o'clock, and it was after half past before I got to the works,' confessed Cora. 'It was not my fault, but, even so, I never guessed he would be waiting outside all that time. You're sure you are none the worse for it?' She turned to the old man, her tone full of solicitude.

'No, of course not.' Nevertheless, the words were followed by a fit of coughing. It was a bronchial tendency which had kept him so much confined to the house during the past months.

'Do you mean you were waiting on those steps all that time?' Bruce asked his grandfather. 'In that wind.'

'Yes. I know it was rather foolish of me but I
185

kept expecting the car to arrive any minute.'

'Why on earth were you so late?' Bruce turned on his wife. 'Why didn't you telephone if you knew you were going to be late?'

'That was just the trouble. I didn't know. My hairdressing appointment should have left me heaps of time, and I should have had if it had not been for that fool of a girl who put me under the hair dryer. She left me there twice as long as usual and I just could not get hold of her. She had put me in one of the private cubicles they still have for those old ladies who don't like having their hair dried in public. I have never been put in one of those before, but the others were all taken. It would be just today of all days. And it would be the day when they put that stupid girl on to me. I was livid, but I could not do anything. If only somebody had come I could have got them to phone, but not a soul came near me.'

It all sounded very genuine, thought Beverley. She had only been in one of those cubicles herself about twice, but she remembered how cut off she had felt. Bruce, lacking that feminine knowledge, was inclined to carp at his wife's explanation.

'Surely you could have got hold of someone,' he protested. 'Don't tell me you have no means of getting in touch with the staff.'

'I suppose I could have come out from under the dryer,' Cora spoke slowly, 'but that never entered my head. Somehow once you are under that dryer you feel as though you have got to stay there until you are released. I don't know why, but it's like that.'

'Sounds cracked to me,' muttered her husband. 'I can't imagine any man putting up with that.'

'Let's forget it.' John Sheavyn felt that too much attention had been focussed on the subject. 'I was the one who was really to blame. I ought to have waited inside. Anyhow no harm has been done.'

The next morning, however, gave the lie to that statement. John Sheavyn did not get up the next day. He had spent a restless night, troubled by constant coughing. By evening, he was far from well and when the doctor was summoned the next day, he pronounced that the bronchitis which he had been fighting all winter had at last won the battle. John Sheavyn was very ill, and he continued to be so for days.

Cora was almost too concerned, too ready to beat her breast in guilt. It was an attitude so foreign to Cora that it aroused all Beverley's suspicions. She wondered how Bruce viewed his wife's over-solicitousness.

'Do let me help nurse Mr. Sheavyn,' she

had cried. 'After all I do feel it is partly my fault.'

The offer received scant approval from Matthew and his wife. 'She'll have him in his grave in no time,' Florence said to Beverley the next morning. Beverley did not know whether there was a double edge to the words, whether Florence meant that Cora's ministrations, though innocent, would have a bad effect on the patient or whether those ministrations would have a definite end in view. Bruce's reaction had no hidden meanings but it was just as definite.

'I think it would be better not, Cora,' he said when his wife made the suggestion. 'Matthew and Florence are used to him and he is used to them. I think it would be a mistake to make any alteration.'

'As you like. I was only trying to be helpful.' Cora was on the point of flouncing out of the room when she recollected herself. This was not the time to undo all her good work of the last days. Mr. Sheavyn's illness brought her chances of being mistress of Willerton Grance all the nearer. She must not alienate Bruce too much. Beverley marvelled at her meek reply. 'Perhaps you are right, Bruce,' she had said. 'Still, if I can help, I will.'

'Thank you, Cora,' Bruce answered gravely. Cora's present behaviour puzzled him. It seemed too good to be true. It was over ten days since she had flown into a temper, since she had flayed him with her sarcastic tongue, and she had even been polite to his grandfather. Why could not she have behaved like this earlier? Though he was grateful for it he knew that it was too late. Love had vanished too thoroughly to be recalled. He even found it hard to think of her kindly in spite of her present behaviour.

Those were days when the whole household waited, waited for what might happen to John Sheavyn. The doctor had said that he might recover or that he might go suddenly. Which way his illness would go no one could say. There came a day when the news was better.

'Two more days, and if nothing goes wrong, he should be out of the wood,' the doctor had said.

It was on the day after this message of hope that Beverley learned that her fears had not been the weavings of an over-active imagination, that they were only too well founded, that her suspicions were rooted in reality. She had, as usual, been in the kitchen for her morning coffee.

'He's sleeping like a baby,' Florence had said proudly. John Sheavyn had slept most of the time during these last days. Those who loved him had hoped that it was a healing sleep, but had feared that it was otherwise, that he was sleeping himself out of life. Now they rejoiced that he slept; this peaceful sleep, so different from the restless tossing of the first days, could only be good.

'I had better be going now,' Beverley had said only a minute or two later.

'What's the hurry?' demanded Florence. 'You've only just swallowed your coffee, and you gulped it at that.'

'I know,' agreed Beverley, 'but I'm behind with my work. I must get this bit finished before I go to London.'

Bruce had readily agreed that she should take a week's holiday at Easter. She had not told him that by doing so she hoped to avoid Gilbert Marrow, but she had told him that this holiday would not prevent her finishing her work in the library by Whitsuntide. The time during which John Sheavyn had been ill had disrupted her schedule. Not only had she done much to make things easier for Matthew and Florence, her offer to sit with the old man at times had been accepted, but she found that the mental worry slowed her work down, but she still hoped to finish by the alloted date.

She was only halfway through the kitchen door when she saw a movement at the end of the corridor. Cora was in the act of closing John Sheavyn's door. Beverley stepped back

190

into the kitchen and waited. Cora glanced round surreptitiously, then turned and went in the direction of her own apartment. Beverley still waited. When she was certain that Cora would be out of sight, she walked slowly in the direction of the old man's flat. Her suspicions had come back twentyfold.

What had Cora Sheavyn been doing in that part of the house? She might of course have been paying a friendly visit, but she knew, as did every other member of the family, that at this time he was almost certain to be asleep, that Florence gave him his morning drink and then settled him for a period of undisturbed rest. Also, if it had been a friendly visit why that surreptitious, searching scanning of the corridors?

Beverley found herself filled with an overwhelming sense of foreboding. She quickened her step, opened the door which Cora had closed so silently but a few seconds ago, and went to John Sheavyn's bedroom. As she opened the door she was met by a blast which almost took her breath away. It was just such another gusty March day as it had been when Cora had been late for her appointment with John Sheavyn and every window in the room was flung wide open. The man in the bed still slept. Beverley rushed across the room and banged the windows down. John

Sheavyn stirred.

'What's that?' he murmured sleepily.

'It's all right, Mr. Sheavyn,' soothed Beverley. 'I was just closing a window.'

'Florence shouldn't have opened them,' he muttered, but he was asleep again within seconds of the last word.

Beverley stood transfixed. She was trembling in every limb. It was Cora who had done this horrible deed, Cora who had intended that the gale which raged through the bedroom should do its dastardly worst and in doing so make her the mistress of Willerton Grange. And Cora would be back before long to close those windows, to remove all traces of her murderous activities, and she would find the windows closed. She would be aware that the person who had closed the windows might possibly, even probably, put the right interpretation on the presence of those open windows. She might comfort herself that the windows could have been opened for a few minutes to air the room, that the finder, whoever it was, might be unsuspecting of malice, but she would not know. Beverley decided that Cora must not find her in, or near, the room, she must not know that it was Beverley who had discovered the open windows. It was she who had thwarted the last attempt at murder—her recent doubts as to the validity of her suspicions had dissolved as rapidly and completely as ice in the sun.

She went to the door, hesitated. There was no sign of Cora. She started towards the library, turned back. If Cora should see her there she might suspect her of having visited Mr. Sheavyn on her way back from her coffee. She could return to her own rooms, but that would be unusual for this time of the day. She must do nothing that was out of her usual routine. That meant she ought still to be in the kitchen and it was there she must return, but to do so would involve her in an explanation. She would have to give Matthew and Florence some reason for her return. And she would give the true one! She could no longer keep the fact of Cora's wicked intentions to herself. Whether she ought to tell Bruce or not she was still undecided, but she must put Matthew and Florence wise as to the peril which threatened Mr. Sheavyn.

'Hello, what. . . ?' Florence looked up from her pastry board. Matthew still sat at the table, his cup of coffee before him. 'What's the matter, Miss Beverley? You look as though you've seen a ghost. Here, Matthew, pour her another cup of coffee.' She pushed Beverley into a chair and brought a cup from the cupboard. 'Drink that,' she commanded, 'and then tell us what's the matter. There's no hurry,' she added, 'take it easy.' Beverley's hand shook so violently that she was unable to lift the cup to her lips. 'It's not the master, is it?' she asked.

'Y-yes, but he is all right now.' She managed to lift the cup up without spilling it. She sipped the hot liquid gratefully. 'I saw Mrs. Bruce coming out of his room.' She went on to tell them what she had found.

'I'll go and see how he is,' Florence bustled towards the door.

'Keep your eyes open,' advised her husband. 'Don't go bumping into Mrs. Bruce.'

'Aye, I'd forgotten that. I'll be careful.' She left the room but her movements were more circumspect this time.

'This isn't the first time, is it?' said Matthew. 'That business with the car was her work, wasn't it?'

'Yes.'

'The wife and I guessed as much.' Matthew pulled out his pipe—he always smoked a pipe after his coffee. He sat ruminating, saying nothing.

'I'm so afraid for Mr. Sheavyn, Matthew.'

'Aye, it's a bad business, but we shall just have to be on the watch.'

'He's all right.' Florence was back again. 'He's as warm as toast.'

'What are we going to do, Florence?' Beverley appealed to the woman. 'Ought we to tell Mr. Bruce?'

'What do you think, Matthew?' Florence passed the question on to her husband. In all practical matters it was Florence who made the decisions, but in those pertaining to the mind, the spirit, she deferred to Matthew.

'I don't think so.' Matthew puffed at his pipe. 'We've no real proof and Mr. Bruce would kick against the thought that his wife had tried to kill his grandfather. He'd have to. And, again, it would be a terrible burden on him and what could he do more than us three? We'll all be on the watch.'

'I shall be away at Easter,' Beverley reminded him.

'Aye, I know, but her brother will be there. I don't feel as though she'll try anything while he's here. He may be a queer stick in some ways but he's no malice in him. I could bet on that.'

'Aye,' chimed in Florence, 'and her ladyship wouldn't like to put herself wrong with him.'

'No,' agreed Beverley. She felt happier now. With both Matthew and Florence alerted she felt that the risk of harm coming to Mr. Sheavyn was now small. She only hoped that if Cora did try again, it would be in such a

195

way that it would be possible to pin the guilt on her. Would she try again? Beverley thought she would. She had made two essays, both of which had failed. Would she say to herself, third time lucky?

CHAPTER ELEVEN

It was the Thursday before Easter. Beverley, in the train on her way to London, sat back in her corner seat and trained her eyes on the passing landscape, seeking the signs of the early spring which had been so thrusting in the surrounding countryside and gardens during the past weeks, trying by this means to keep her innermost thoughts at bay, to push into the background the words which she had overheard last night. Was it because she was living in a large house, where people naturally thought there was room enough to live their own lives, that she was always overhearing things which were not meant for her ears? This was the third time in these months at Willerton Grange that she had been an eavesdropper, willingly or unwillingly, and each of these times the subject had been, or so it had appeared to her, of sinister import.

Until last evening she had viewed her coming visit to London with mixed feelings. She was naturally pleased at the prospect of seeing Sandra, she was also looking forward to London itself. For a few days it would be fun to be in a large city again though she had known recently that she would no longer care to live there. It was the idea of leaving Willerton Grange which plunged her thoughts into such a turmoil. She knew herself to be as much in love with Bruce as ever but she had been conscious of a very definite constraint in their relations lately, and the constraint was not only on her side. Bruce no longer sought her out, rather he avoided her. When they were thrown together conversation no longer flowed easily between them. To be in the same house with him was no more the joy which it had been once. She was glad also to be leaving behind her the problem of Cora, of Cora's barely hidden resentment towards her, and still more the threat which she offered to John Sheavyn.

'I'm going to forget it all for a week,' she had told herself, knowing as she said it that she was promising herself the unattainable. She would not be able to help worrying about John Sheavyn, wondering whether Cora might not succeed in getting past the Bensons' vigilance. She had the all-too-common feeling that nobody could do the job as well as herself, that if she were not on hand to watch out disaster would overtake the old man. And she knew it would be no more easy to forget Bruce Sheavyn, to rid herself of the longing for him which had become such a part of her.

That had been her reaction until last

evening. Now she was not only still more fearful for John Sheavyn's safety, she was infinitely puzzled about Bruce. Was he the man she thought he was, the man she loved and admired, the man who would be horrified beyond measure if he had any idea of his wife's nefarious schemes, or did he really know about these attempts on his grandfather's life and condone them? She could not believe it, could not believe that Bruce was really a villain, yet what other interpretation could she put on what she had heard last night? She had lain awake long into the night, tossing and turning, trying to find some explanation but she was still as far away as ever.

It had been shortly before dinner when she had heard Cora's voice just outside the library door. The door was open—she had opened it only a few minutes earlier intending to go to her own room to change, and had then remembered a point she had overlooked. She had been about to make a second attempt to leave the library when Cora's voice arrested her.

'Well, and what did he say?'

Beverley's first and natural instinct had been to close the library door, not to eavesdrop on a conversation between husband and wife, but something had stopped her. Was it because Bruce was coming down from his grandfather's rooms so that Cora's question must apply to the old man, and any query about Mr. Sheavyn from Cora was suspect?

'Nothing much, he hasn't really any ideas to offer.'

'Well, that's it then. I warn you, Bruce, I'm going to stop at nothing if that man does not go and he knows it too. I've shown him that already.'

Beverley did not wait to hear more. She closed the door very quietly and stood leaning against it. She was trembling in every limb. How she wished she had shut that door after the very first words—as she ought to have done. It wasn't a case of listeners never hearing any good of themselves, it was worse. If she had not listened she could still have gone on believing Bruce to be innocent of any knowledge of the attempts on his grandfather's life. How could she believe that now? Surely there was no other possible construction to be put on this but that which had immediately leapt to her mind. Cora must have sent her husband to ask when his grandfather was going to retire. She could not see why his retirement should be so important to Cora, but it seemingly was. She must have plans for the works, plans which could not be put into operation as long as John Sheavyn was at the head of the firm—and plans which her husband knew about! As he also knew how important those plans were to his wife, but that was not the worst. He not only knew that she would stop at nothing—and in the light of past events that was murder—but he must also know of past attempts. What else could Cora's words imply?

She had felt unable to go into dinner that day, she could not sit through a meal with Bruce, knowing that she was accusing him thus in her mind. She pleaded a bad headache and asked that Matthew should bring something to her room. Long before she went to bed, the excuse had become fact. Her thoughts went to and fro with the regularity of a pendulum, reaching one unassailable fact and back again to another, never breaking the pattern, never coming through with a new idea. The sight of Bruce the next morning had done nothing to change the pattern, it had only exaggerated the tragedy of it. He had appeared at the front door just as she was setting off. She had already said goodbye to his grandfather.

'Goodbye, Beverley,' he had said. He seemed brighter, more friendly than he had been latterly. 'Have a good time. We shall look forward to seeing you back next Friday.'

It was completely inexplicable. What sort of a man was Bruce Sheavyn? She could have sworn that he was very fond of his grandfather. Was there a basic weakness somewhere, a weakness which made it possible for his wife to swing him over to her point of view, even to the extent of conniving at crime? She thought of Lady Macbeth. Cora was just such another. Had she the same power over her husband? Beverley discovered that she was no longer cognisant of anything beyond the window. Her thoughts were all turned inwards, or rather they were turned on Bruce, the man whom she still loved whatever he was, even if he was the weakling she had now come to suspect. The word weakling no sooner took harbourage in her mind than she pushed it out angrily. That word and everything that she knew about Bruce were miles apart. Bruce a weakling who would sit by and watch his own grandfather murdered! It was as incredible as that the river Lune, over which she was passing at that moment, should suddenly turn and flow back into the mountains. She knew that she was young, immature, that her judgment was far from infallible, that in this case, she was undoubtedly biased, but nevertheless her whole being cried out against the picture of Bruce Sheavyn which she had been trying to draw.

'Oh, drop it,' she apostrophised herself

silently. 'Let it simmer. You are only getting more and more tied up.' Resolutely she forced herself to look, with seeing eyes, at the passing landscape, to be awake to the signs of this early spring. At Arnside, in the Lake District, the signs had been everywhere. The gardens were aglow with daffodils; the other flowers of early spring, less showy but equally welcome, contributed their modest share to the panorama of the unfolding spring, and the almond blossom and forsythia added their quota of colour to the green which was just beginning to tinge the trees and hedgerows. The latter were alive with all the tiny omens of life to come and, perhaps the most prevalent sign of all in that district, the lambs were everywhere, wandering at will over the hillsides. Seen from the train, even though she was going south where spring came earlier, the signs were much less evident. One had to get close to nature at this time of the year to see its promise.

'Beverley!' The long journey was over. By dint of concentration on the view beyond the window and the idiosyncrasies of her fellow travellers she had succeeded in keeping a certain rein on her troubling thoughts. Now, at the sight of Sandra in her bright green mini skirt, they vanished—for the time being. It was good to see Sandra again, to be the recipient of her uninhibited, joyous welcome.

'What does it feel like being engaged?' They were hardly out of the station when Beverley put the question. She was genuinely interested but, also, she intended to be the aggressor as far as questions were concerned. She was not yet sure how much she wanted to tell her friend of her own concerns.

'Smashing! You'll have to do the same yourself. What about this Bruce Sheavyn? Is he as nice as you thought?'

'Yes, but he's married. I told you that in my letters.'

'Oh, that! It doesn't always make that much difference these days, does it?' Sandra brushed the objection lightly aside. Beverley wished she could dispose of it as easily. 'Has he fallen for you?'

'He has not.' The denial was emphatic but there was a bleakness inside the girl as she made it. 'You know I went away on purpose to be rid of all that sort of thing.' Did she say this to convince herself or Sandra?

'Maybe, but that doesn't mean to say you have.' Their arrival at the hostel prevented Sandra from enlarging on this subject. Miss Horsfall was in the hall as they entered.

'Beverley Gordon!' she exclaimed. 'You are looking well. Do you like your new work?' she asked. She had often wondered about

Beverley; enquiries from her friend had elicited little real information.

They went up to Sandra's room. Beverley stood and stared. Had it always been as bad as this? Had it always been so shabby, so dingy, or was it that she was seeing it through new eyes, contrasting it with the pleasant rooms which were hers at Willerton Grange?

'Thinking how different it all is from your own palatial apartment?' mocked Sandra.

Beverley blushed. She did not know she had been so obvious. 'I suppose I was,' she confessed. 'It's amazing how quickly one gets used to living in luxury.'

'Well, we are going to let you down gently,' Sandra consoled her. 'Laurie is going to take us out to a meal and a show tonight.'

The next four days flew. Laurie and Sandra had decided that relations were out for this holiday—both sets of relations had been visited during Christmas and the New Year. For this holiday they were staying in London, but going to the coast daily. Laurie had a car, hardly a Rolls-Royce but roadworthy enough for all normal purposes. Beverley had protested that they would not want her with them all the time but they had assured her otherwise. She had insisted that they have Sunday to themselves and had arranged to visit another friend that day.

She got to know Laurie during those days and came to the conclusion that he and Sandra were well suited, that they complemented each other. He was level-headed, rather serious, but with sufficient sense of humour to be able to appreciate his fiancée's sallies and to give as good as he got. Beverley found that she liked him and was able to rejoice in Sandra's good fortune, though not without a certain inward envy.

It was not until her last evening in London that Beverley unburdened herself to any degree. It had been comparatively easy to keep the conversation about her life at Willerton Grange on an impersonal level. Until that evening she had hardly been alone with Sandra. Laurie had always been one of the party and they had arrived back at the hostel so late that they had both been too tired to talk much. On that last evening, however, Sandra had told Laurie that the pattern was to be changed and that she wanted to have Beverley to herself.

'I just don't know anything about how things really are with you,' she had declared. 'You've been a real clam. I've done all the talking.' It was quite true. Sandra had been more than ready to talk of her future, of the date of the wedding—it was fixed for the following September—of their plans for a house, of the furniture which had been promised them, of that which they would have to buy. So, after dinner on the Wednesday she shepherded Beverley upstairs and planted her in one of the 'easy' chairs—so different from the counterparts in Beverley's room at Willerton Grange. 'Now talk,' Sandra ordered.

Beverley laughed. 'What about?' she asked.

'Everything. Tell me what they are all like. I only know about the place so far. Tell me about the people.'

Beverley complied with reservations, but as the evening wore on she settled back into her old easy relationship with the other girl. She found herself telling of Cora, of her attempts on John Sheavyn's life. What she did not tell her was of that last overheard conversation, of the possibility that Bruce Sheavyn might be aware of his wife's perfidy.

'Coo, it's like a detective story, or one of those Sherlock Holmes tales on television.' Sandra had listened open-eyed, nearly open-mouthed. 'Weren't you afraid to leave him with only those two old people to guard him?' Sandra was one of those young people who thought that anybody over fifty was almost doddering, certainly unable to cope with a situation such as her friend had been describing.

'I was, a bit, but Matthew and Florence are very good. I'm quite sure they won't let Cora get away with anything. At least I'm nearly sure, but I shall be relieved to get home and know that everything is all right.'

'Home?' Sandra noted the word. 'Does it feel like home to you?'

'Yes, it does.' Beverley had not realised it until Sandra put the question, but she knew now that it was more home to her than anything she had known for a long time. More home than her own home had been during the latter years of her mother's life.

'What about Bruce Sheavyn? You've hardly mentioned him.'

'What do you want me to say? He is very nice, very kind, and he is giving me a job in his works when the library is finished, at least it was old Mr. Sheavyn who suggested it.' What had made her say this? She thought she had decided not to take that job.

'Where are the works?'

'In Kendal.'

'And are you going into rooms in Kendal? That will be a bit of a change, won't it?'

'I am not going into rooms. Mr. Sheavyn has asked me to stay on at the Grange.' Once more she was speaking in direct contradiction to what she had decided.

'Which Mr. Sheavyn? Bruce?'

'No!' Beverley spoke sharply. 'Old Mr. Sheavyn. There's nothing like you're trying to make out. Mr. Sheavyn asked me and one of the reasons he gave was that he enjoyed my company. I play chess with him.'

'And what about Bruce?' Seemingly Sandra could not let the subject drop.

'Oh, you are impossible.' Beverley got up from her chair. 'It's time I started packing.' Sandra's needling was too near the truth for comfort.

'Tra-la. Methinks the lady doth protest too much. Pipe down, Beverley,' as the other opened her lips to protest. 'I won't say any more, but we shall see what we shall see,' the last words in sepulchral tones.

'Yes, we shall,' retorted Beverley, but she was glad to let the matter rest there.

She left London the next morning with little regret. It had been nice to see Sandra, to indulge in the easy badinage which had always been a feature of their friendship, and it had been a relief to have her thoughts occupied with matters which had nothing to do with Willerton Grange. Not that those other matters had afforded a complete barrage to the other, but they had given her a breathing space, an opportunity to sit back and take a saner view. Her motto now was the Asquithian 'wait and see'. She would await developments, on the watch, but withholding judgment until such time, if ever, when she would know more.

As the train took her further and further north the more excited she became. She was going home. Yes, she was going home, she thought more soberly, but to what was she returning? Would she find John Sheavyn still more advanced on the way to good health or would some further mishap have befallen him? As the train slowed down at Arnside, she put her head out of the window, wondering who would meet her. She had no doubt that there would be someone. Bruce had enquired the time of her return before she left. Gilbert Marrow! She could have cried with disappointment.

'Cora was coming to meet you,' he said, 'but at the last minute one of her flower club members got on the phone to her so I said I would come.'

'I thought you said you were going home yesterday.' Beverley blurted the words out without thinking. She had been so convinced that her plan to avoid Gilbert Marrow had been successful. His presence by her side proved too much for her manners and her wariness.

'So I was, but I decided to stay another couple of days so that I could see you. Not that

I told Cora that, but I was quite upset when I found that you had gone away. You have not forgotten what we said in the library, have you?'

'What you said,' she retorted.

'Same thing.' He opened the car door for her and himself went round to the driving seat. 'Now for it,' he said. He started the car but turned in the opposite direction from that for Willerton Grange.

'You are going the wrong way,' Beverley told him.

'Oh, no, I'm not. You and I are going for a little drive first.'

'We're not,' she said angrily. 'I want to go straight home.'

'Calm down.' He patted her knee. 'We are not going far. Just to a nice little quiet place I know.'

Beverley sat and fumed. She was powerless. There was nothing she could do short of knocking Gilbert out. She could only hope that her ramrod-like back, her heavy silence would convince the man that his attentions were really unwelcome.

'Here we are.' He pulled the car on to the grassy bank of a tree-shaded lane. 'We shan't be interrupted here. This lane only leads to the farm.' He turned to her and bent over to kiss her. She pushed her hand flat against his face.

'Come, Beverley.' He looked quite hurt. He had jerked his head away and grasped both her hands in his. 'Don't be a little fool. It's no use pretending you are averse to a little love-making. If you are you're the first girl I've met like that.'

'Well, I am the first girl then.'

'Sez you.' He bent over her once more. She struggled, pulling this way and that, trying in vain to free her hands. In desperation she sank her teeth deep into his wrists. He drew back quickly, releasing her hands.

'You little wildcat!' He stared at her, sucking his wrist. 'You really did mean it.' He turned to the wheel, and without another word backed the car down the lane. It was not until they turned into the drive of Willerton Grange that he spoke again.

'I'm sorry,' he said. 'I wouldn't have done it if I had thought you really meant it.'

'You needed a lot of telling,' she said grimly.

'Y-yes.' He hesitated. 'Don't let on to Cora, will you? She would only be mad with us both,' he said as she got out of the car.

'No, nor you.' She left him and ran up the stairs to her own room. How good it was to be back—in spite of Gilbert Marrow. How cosy her sitting-room looked. How different it was from Sandra's room and how welcoming was

212

the blazing fire on the hearth. A far cry from the popping, complaining gas fire which she had left.

'I must go and see Matthew and Florence,' she said to herself. She threw her coat on the bed and went down to the kitchen.

'Miss Beverley! It's good to see you.'

'Well, and how's London? Did you have a good time?'

Matthew and Florence spoke in one breath.

'Yes, thank you, but it's nice to be back. How are you both?'

'Oh, we're all right.' It was Florence who answered. 'I won't ask you to have a cup of tea,' they were sitting at the table drinking tea, 'her ladyship has sent a message saying as you're to have tea with her.'

'Oh.'

'Yes, it is "oh", isn't it? She's been on her best behaviour while you've been away. Butter wouldn't melt in her mouth. Makes you think, doesn't it?'

'She's had her brother here, Florence,' Matthew reminded her. 'That always puts her in a good temper.'

'Aye, but she's been better than usual. Still, let's be thankful for small mercies.'

'And Mr. Sheavyn? Is he all right?' That question had been on the tip of her tongue as she hung out of the carriage at Arnside, but

213

Gilbert Marrow's behaviour had sent it flying, and once that episode had terminated she had not felt like asking Gilbert Marrow anything.

'Right as a cricket. At least he's very well considering. He's even been out for a few short walks. And as I told you, no trouble from her ladyship.'

'Good! I have been worrying.'

As she returned to her rooms she pondered over Cora's exemplary behaviour. Was there anything behind it or was she really turning over a new leaf? She was still undecided when Cora's entrance and her subsequent conversation puzzled her still more.

'Hello, Beverley,' she greeted her. 'Gilbert told me you had arrived. Will you come and have a cup of tea with us?'

'Thank you, Cora. I should like to.' As Florence had said, butter would not have melted in her mouth. Silly expression that, thought the girl. What did it really matter? Whatever it meant there was little doubt that Cora was putting herself out to be pleasant. Absence makes the heart grow fonder? wondered Beverley. She talked in a friendly manner for a few minutes, asking Beverley about her holiday.

'Well, I will leave you to your unpacking. Don't be many minutes.'

'No, I'll be along in a few seconds,'

promised Beverley.

She did not wait to put her clothes away, but merely washed her hands and brushed her hair before following Cora. When she reached the landing Cora was disappearing along the corridor and Bruce was coming out of the library.

'Beverley!' Bruce's face lit up as he looked towards the staircase and caught sight of Beverley above him.

'Hello, Bruce.' What a joy to know that Bruce was so pleased to see her. What a lovely home-coming this was. She started to run down the stairs. Her toe caught in something. She felt herself falling, falling. She made a grab at the stair-rail, but she was falling. There was a sudden excruciating pain in the region of her ankle. She found herself in Bruce's arms. He was staggering to maintain his balance. He backed against the wall for support. Suddenly his arms tightened convulsively about her, his lips were pressed passionately against hers. She felt her own response. For a second the pain in her ankle was forgotten, driven out by a stronger emotion. In a second it was all over.

CHAPTER TWELVE

Everything happened at once then. Bruce pushed her away from him as though he had been stung. Cora came running back down the corridor.

'What's happened? What are you doing home at this time, Bruce? What's the matter with Beverley?' When Bruce had pushed her from him Beverley had collapsed on the floor. She tried to rise now, but sank back with a stifled groan.

'My foot,' she murmured.

'I'm sorry.' Bruce seemed to be coming out of a daze. 'Did I hurt you?'

'No, it wasn't you. I felt it as I was falling.'

'But what has happened?' asked Cora again. 'Did Beverley fall downstairs?'

'She did.' Bruce bent over Beverley and lifted her from the ground. 'Can you stand if I hold you?' he asked. His face was as white as Beverley's.

'Yes.' She gave a grimace as she tried to take a step. Bruce made as though to pick her up but, flushing, changed his tactics.

'Put your hand on my shoulder,' he said, 'and try to hop.' He turned to his wife. 'Go and fetch Florence, will you, Cora?' He guided

Beverley gently into the library, helping her into a chair. 'We'll let Florence have a look at it first. She is very hot on first aid. We can send for the doctor after she's seen it.'

'Tumbling downstairs, Miss Beverley!' Florence came bustling in, Cora at her heels. 'And you hadn't even had a cup of tea, not to mention anything stronger.' She knelt down by Beverley, eased off her shoe, gently removed her stocking. 'Just a bad strain,' she said after feeling it carefully. 'Hot and cold water, that's what you want. But you'll have to keep off it.' Florence took command. 'We'd better get you up to your rooms and then you can stay there for a day or two. There'll be no need for you to try and go up and down stairs. We can bring your meals up to you. That'll be best, won't it, Mr. Bruce?' She turned to Bruce, suddenly realising that the master of the house might wish to have some say in the arrangements.

'Yes, Florence,' agreed Bruce. 'I'll help her upstairs,' he offered, as Florence made to help the girl to her feet. 'You go and get your hot and cold contraptions ready.'

Florence bustled off and Bruce helped Beverley to her feet and began the slow journey upstairs.

'Come along for your tea as soon as you have got Beverley upstairs,' said Cora. 'I hope

Maureen has not brought it in already or it will be stone cold. I'll go and see about it.'

'There!' Bruce lowered Beverley into a chair. 'I hope that wasn't too painful.'

'Hardly at all, thank you.' Beverley felt that she might have been talking to a stranger. Bruce had not spoken a word as he helped her mount the stairs. His touch had been completely impersonal: he had moved stiffly as though he was afraid that any natural movement might betray him. Betray what? Feelings that he was trying to stifle? Certainly the automaton that accompanied her into her room was oceans away from the man into whose arms she had catapulted, the man whose lips had sought hers with such passion.

'Well, I will leave you to Florence now.' He turned on his heels as the woman entered the room, laden with a tray containing bowls, cloths and bandaging. It was as though he had no further interest.

'What really happened?' Florence was crouching by Beverley's side, applying hot and cold fomentations in rapid succession. 'What were you doing to fall downstairs?'

'Something tripped me up.'

'Something tripped you up? What?'

'I could have sworn there was a rope across the stairs, but there was no sign of it when I came upstairs.' She had specially noted this on

218

the return journey, had looked for the offending rope.

'There wouldn't be,' Florence sniffed. 'She's had plenty of time to remove it.'

So Florence thought the same. Beverley was convinced that it had been put there purposely by Cora. For some reason or other—possibly it was part of her campaign against John Sheavyn—Beverley had got to be removed from the scene.

'What do we do now?' she asked.

'Nothing. We can't. There's no evidence. It's like all the other times—those attempts on Mr. Sheavyn. She's too clever. Still, give her enough rope and she'll hang herself.'

'If she doesn't hang somebody else first. Heaven knows what would have happened to me if Mr. Bruce had not been there.'

Bruce Sheavyn was thinking the same thing. He sat in the same room as his wife and brother-in-law, drinking tea with them, but though he managed to give the occasional reply to their remarks, his thoughts were not with them. They were going round and round, milling over that disastrous kiss, for disastrous he felt it to have been. Not because he had broken his word to Beverley—he had told her at the interview that she need not fear that sort of treatment from him—but because it had shown him how little control he had over his own actions. He did not try to hide from himself that he was deeply in love with Beverley—all his evasive tactics of the last weeks had availed nothing—but it was a love that could get nowhere. There was no point in putting his fortunes to the test as far as his wife was concerned. He knew that Cora would not contemplate the prospect of divorcing him. To ask would only add one more weapon to her armoury of aggressiveness. By that kiss he had not only betrayed his feelings to Beverley but he stood self-revealed in his own inability to cope—for the present at least. If only he had not come home early—it had been necessary to see someone in Arnside at half past three and had not been worth going back—this would never have happened. But Beverley would have tumbled down the stairs whether he had been there or not and if he had not been there what might not have happened? A deep sigh escaped him.

'What's the matter, old man?' Gilbert had not failed to notice his brother-in-law's withdrawnness.

'Sorry.' Bruce tried to bring his thoughts back to his companions. 'Just some trouble at the works,' he lied.

The answer satisfied Gilbert but Cora was not deceived. She had not seen what had occurred but she guessed his present self-absorption had its origin in the recent episode. Cora, though she was putting up a better show than her husband, was also troubled. It would seem that there was a jinx on all her plans. They all went astray. It was because of the previous fiasco that she had tried to eliminate Beverley. She did not know who had closed the windows in her father-in-law's room and so foiled her last attempt, but it might have been Beverley, and Beverley had certainly been the one who turned the car away from the old man when she had made her first try. It was more than possible that Beverley Gordon suspected her intentions though she had shown no signs of it. Therefore, if she was ever to succeed, and without drawing suspicion to herself, Beverley must be got rid of. Not necessarily killed, she told herself. She did not really want to kill the girl—though it was strange how once one had thought of such a thing murder did not seem to matter very much. As far as Mr. Sheavyn was concerned, she had now no qualms of conscience. She had accustomed herself to the idea and, after all he was old, he had lived his life. Everybody said that it was no fun being old so she was really doing him no great disservice, but it was different with Beverley. She had her life before her. Still she had got to be moved from Willerton Grange by some means.

'I wonder what on earth made Beverley fall downstairs.' Bruce put his cup down and prepared to leave the room.

'Joy at seeing you.' Cora could not deny herself this cut. 'She had not seen you for over a week.'

'Don't talk such rot, Cora.' Bruce strode angrily from the room. Cora was too adept at putting her finger on the sore spot.

'Poor old Bruce.' She looked after her husband, a malicious smile playing round her lips. 'He can't bear to be teased.'

'You can go too far, Cora,' warned her brother, thinking of his own recent fray with Beverley Gordon.

'Oh, I know what I am doing.' It was not only malice that had prompted her remark. By taking the war into the enemy's country she had diverted her husband's attention from her own activities, not that Bruce could possibly have any idea as to what had caused Beverley to stumble. As it had transpired it had been child's play to smuggle that rope away. She had moved it as she went to fetch Florence and removed it completely while Bruce had taken the patient upstairs and Florence gone off to the kitchen. Nothing could have worked out more satisfactorily. The only person who could have any suspicion was Beverley, and Cora was pretty sure she would not say anything. What possible evidence could she produce to uphold her accusation. Still, she would have to be very careful for a while. Her luck might not hold another time. She must keep a weather eye open for Beverley.

For the time being, however, Beverley needed no weather eye trained on her. Solitary confinement, she thought to herself when Florence had left her with a tea tray by her side. This lovely homecoming had taken a wrong turning. She had almost forgotten while she was in London that life at Willerton Grange had its problems. It had presented her with an unexpected one when Gilbert Marrow had met her at the station, but she had succeeded in tackling that. The others had faded into nothing after Florence's reassuring words and the sight of Bruce's welcoming smile. They had returned in full force now, supported by a new horde of invading troubles. Not only was Mr. Sheavyn in danger from Cora but she, herself, had been put on the killer's list.

Then there was the trouble about Bruce. That kiss! It was bitter-sweet. The ecstasy of the moment had left its aftermath of torment, mingled though it was with a joy she could not suppress, the joy of the knowledge that not only did she love Bruce but that that love was returned. The knowledge itself was two-edged. Believing that the love was on her part only she had been able to persuade herself that there was no valid reason for her to leave Willerton Grange, no valid cause why she should not accept the offered post at John Sheavyn's works. Those words blurted out to Sandra must have been the result of subconscious workings of her mind and the very uttering of them had crystallised her decision that she would stay on at Willerton Grange.

Everything was altered now. Even if she herself did not reverse that decision, Bruce Sheavyn would do it for her. He had made it very plain that the kiss was not to be taken to mean anything. What else could he do? she asked herself. He was a married man and a man of principles. It was true that there were odd moments when she did wonder if it was love that lay behind that kiss, whether it had not been just another of those male philanderings but every particle of her being told her that this was not so, and this being the case, what else could he do? He would have to send her away. If he were not married it would have been different, but he was married. How soon would he tell her to go? Not until her ankle was better.

'I've brought you something to read.' Bruce had not brought an answer to her question, but he had brought the wherewithal to sidetrack her troubles temporarily. 'I've brought you the latest Winston Graham and Alexander Cordell's *Sinews of Love*. They will help to pass the time while you are kept a prisoner.'

'Oh, thank you, Bruce.' She wondered whether he would sit down and if he did what he would say, but if he had anything to say to her he was obviously not going to say it yet. He was gone before the last words of thanks had left her lips. Very un-Bruce-like behaviour, at least the Bruce of the early days of their acquaintance.

She did manage to keep her worries at bay for a time. Not only was she able to lose herself in her reading but when Matthew came to clear her tea he told her that Mr. Sheavyn had suggested that he come up for a game of chess that evening. So it was not going to be a case of solitary confinement. She was going to have visitors. As it turned out, every member of the house visited her from time to time. Even Gilbert came in to say 'goodbye' before he departed for home.

'Sorry about your ankle, Beverley,' he had said, standing awkwardly by her chair. 'By the way, we'll forget all about yesterday, shall we?'

'Yes.' Beverley knew she would not forget,

but at least she would keep it to herself.

'Cora will be coming up to see you when she gets back from taking me to the station,' said her brother. 'She asked me to tell you.'

Cora! What would Cora have to say to her. She must know that Beverley guessed that it was she who had put that rope across the stairs. But Cora when she came could not have been more innocent-seeming.

'What a bind for you, Beverley,' she had exclaimed. 'And just after all your holiday. Tell me all about London. What is London like these days? I really must go down soon. The trouble is that when Bruce goes there it is for such a short time that he says that it is not worth my going. I rather suspect he does not want me to go with him. If he stayed longer I should say he'd got somebody else up there, but he doesn't stay long enough for that.'

Beverley had no reply to this. She guessed that Cora knew as well as she did that Bruce was hardly the sort of man to have a mistress in London, or anywhere else. Instead Beverley concentrated on Cora's first request. She told her, to the best of her ability, about London, though she surmised that her London would be very different from Cora's.

In spite of her incarceration, it was not the days that went slowly for Beverley. It was the nights which seemed so endless. It was at

226

night that her ankle ached and it was during the nights that she had time to ponder on her position, to wonder how long it would be before Bruce gave her her notice and what would she do then. Should she go back to London and take an ordinary job there? After all, she had learned much while she was here. She had learned that she was just like other girls, that she wanted nothing more than to be loved by someone. True she wanted that someone to be Bruce, but since it could not be, she would have to try to be content with a second best. What she had discovered was that she no longer wanted to avoid the opposite sex. The question was now how long would it be before circumstances, in the shape of Bruce Sheavyn, forced her to seek a post elsewhere. Would he want her to go before she finished the library?

It was on Tuesday that Bruce next came to see her. He had sent up some more books by Matthew in the meantime but had not come himself.

'Can I come in, Beverley?' He came and sat down by the fire. 'I just came to let you know that I am going to London for a couple of nights. Don't try to get down to the library before I get back.'

'But I intended starting tomorrow,' she protested. 'My ankle is much better and I am sure I could easily manage the stairs now.'

'Don't try. There's no hurry.'

'But . . .' He silenced her.

'The skies won't fall down if you are a day or two behind your schedule,' he told her. 'Goodness knows you have had little enough break since you came. Give it a rest until I come back.' His journey to London was of no immediate urgency, but he had seized upon it as a perfect delaying tactic. He hoped that distance would give him a chance to get his thoughts into perspective, that he might be able to come to some decision about his future actions unhindered by the distraction of Beverley's too near presence. He did not know that, less than a week ago Beverley had expected London to accomplish for her the same therapeutic miracle.

Beverley spent those next two days in accustoming her ankle to normal usage once more. She was amazed at the speed of its recovery.

'Oh, there's nothing like hot and cold,' Florence had said when Beverley expressed her surprise. 'Get at it right away and it works wonders.'

On the day Bruce was expected home, Beverley set out for a short walk immediately after lunch. The more gentle exercise she took the sooner, she felt, would her ankle be

228

thoroughly strong. She was just in sight of the end of the drive when Bruce's car turned in. He drew up beside her.

'Hello, how's the ankle?' he asked.

'Fine,' she answered. 'I'm going for a walk now to give it a bit of practice.'

'What about coming down to the boat with me? I'm just going in to change and then I'm going down to the club. What are the others doing?' he asked.

'Cora has gone in to Kendal for some meeting and your grandfather is resting.'

'Good! Then that leaves us free. Would you like to come to the boat?'

'Yes, I should. What should I wear? Are we likely to go sailing or are we just going to look at it?'

'Primarily to look at it. I thought that if it should be a decent day tomorrow we might all go for a sail. I did look her over while you were in London but I thought I'd go down this afternoon and make sure everything was all right. We might go for a short sail if it is. Wear slacks and a warm jersey.'

Beverley hurried up to her room to change, rejoicing at the change in Bruce's attitude. He was almost his old friendly self. She wondered what could have happened in London to bring about this transformation.

Nothing had happened in London. It was

merely that, as he had hoped, Bruce Sheavyn had succeeded in the anonymity of the big city, away from all his home associations, in coming to terms with himself, to look at things from an unbiased point of view. He had decided that the situation in which he had found himself was not unmanageable, that he was sufficiently strong-minded to conquer this thing which had struck him—now that he knew what it was. He would have to watch himself, he would have to watch Beverley, and he must not have Beverley working in the same office, but that did not mean that Beverley must not work at Sheavyn's. His first all-pervading thought had been that he must not punish Beverley Gordon for his own weakness. Whatever happened, he must not turn Beverley off—at least not yet. If the situation did get beyond his control he might have to act later but at present he must keep his promise that the girl should be employed at Sheavyn's, but he could alter the conditions of working. He would tell her that he had come to the conclusion that before working with him it would be best to get a thorough working knowledge of the works in all departments. Once having come to this decision he had been able to concentrate on his own position and had worked through to a state of near peace and confidence.

'Ready?' Bruce was already in the car when Beverley came down dressed in grey slacks and a deep blue pullover. She had bought the pullover in London during her recent holiday and was very pleased with her purchase. Bruce wished that his companion looked less attractive.

'Isn't it heavenly?' As the car took the familiar road to Arnside, Beverley felt that she was indeed having a foretaste of heaven. Bruce was by her side, cheerful and chatty, the sun was shining, the countryside was burgeoning with spring. The last weeks had transformed the landscape. The hedges were faintly green, the orchards were white with blossom. Hope was in the air, hope was once more alive in Beverley's heart.

'By the way, you do swim, don't you?' They were driving along the almost deserted front when Bruce shot this question at her.

'Yes, quite well.'

Bruce's question had come only a second prior to his stopping the car, giving her no time to expatiate on her swimming prowess— it was considerable—had she so desired. He left the car at the end of the main promenade—if it could be dignified by such a title—and led her along the narrower walk, skirting a garden wall.

'There she is. George has got her out.' They

231

had reached the cove where several yachts lay moored. Bruce went to one lying quite near to the water's edge, one with sails of a deep blue. 'Did you get your pullover to match the sails?' he laughed.

'I might have done, mightn't I? Only I did not even know that your boat had blue sails.'

'Isn't she a beauty?' Bruce ran his hands lovingly along the boat's sides.

'Yes. I don't know what constitutes a beauty in a boat. I don't know a thing about yachts, but she certainly looks good.'

'Take my word for it, she is. George!' A grey-haired old sailor who had been tinkering with another boat came slowly towards them. 'How is she? Is everything O.K.?'

'Yes, Mr. Bruce. She's in fine trim. I went over her again after you'd finished and there was nothing wrong at all. She's ready for the water whenever you want to go.'

'Fine! I think we'll go for a short sail now. What do you say, Beverley?' He began to pull the boat into the water. Beverley added her efforts to his, though she felt they were more of a gesture than a help.

'You would like to crew for me, Beverley, wouldn't you?' he asked as he raised the sails. 'I'm not pushing you into it, am I?'

'No, I would like to try as long as you remember that I hardly know the front of a boat from the back.'

'The fore and the aft,' he laughed. 'You'll soon learn, but I'll let you be a passenger until we get out into the bay. The estuary is a bit tricky. It can be very shallow in parts. I remember when I was a youngster we got stuck on the sandbanks by Holme Island there,' he pointed to a wooded island to their right. 'We were in a rowing boat that time. We often used to take a boat to go picnicking, sometimes there and other times to White Creek or New Barns,' indicating two bays on the mainland, 'and that time we forgot all about the tides and were stranded for hours. By the way, I had better teach you a little of the nautical language. This sail I am holding is the mainsail, and that one in front is the jib. When we get further out I am going to put you in charge of that. That's the beginner's job.'

The wooded shores grew further and further away from them and they finally found themselves in Morecambe Bay. Bruce initiated his companion into the mysteries of managing the jib sail. Beverley clutched it as though her life depended on it. In spite of her 'new boy' feeling she was enjoying herself immensely. As the yacht tacked this way and that, running with the wind as much as possible, Bruce told her, she was filled with a sense of exhilaration, began to long for the time when she, too, would be able to sail the boat, when she could take Bruce's place at the helm, could manipulate the ropes which governed the mainsail.

'Duck!' called Bruce as he swung the great boom round 'That's called gybing,' he explained, 'and everyone on board has got to look out when that happens or they might get a nasty crack.'

So it went on throughout the time they were on the water, Bruce teaching, explaining, initiating her into the nautical phraseology. Beverley proved an apt pupil and also discovered that she was a sailor. She had been nervous as to her own seaworthiness. She had heard much of sea-sickness and had wondered if she would be one of those who suffered it, but there had been never a qualm. She felt she could have gone on for ever and protested when Bruce decreed that they should make for land.

'Enough for the first time, I think,' he had answered. 'Besides, I don't want to overdo that ankle. We'll come out again tomorrow and then you can have a go at running her yourself. You're shaping very well. Cora will be glad. She would far rather be a passenger than have to crew for me, and my grandfather is too old for it now.'

Beverley found herself that night praying

for a fine day on the morrow. Her only other wish was that both Cora and Mr. Sheavyn might find it in their hearts to decide that they did not want to sail, that she might have another sail such as this had been, alone with Bruce.

CHAPTER THIRTEEN

Beverley woke early the next morning. Immediately her thoughts flew to the coming day. What was the weather going to be? Last night's forecast had been far from cheering, but she had consoled herself with the thought that they were often wrong. Alas! They appeared to be only too right this time. The sky was a dull, all-over grey. As she pushed open the window an icy blast met her. She shivered and banged the window shut once more. Beyond it the trees tossed and writhed as though twisted in the grip of some avenging demon. There would be no sailing today. The weather was back into the pattern which had been so prevalent since spring had made its official entry. It was as though the weather god had repented of his earlier leniency, that he was exacting payment for his remission of winter's ills. There had been odd days the last month when it had seemed that he had relented, but they were immediately snatched away, lost in the everlasting grey skies, the cold, biting winds. Yesterday, for a short time, there had been a softening. This morning winter was back.

Those few hours alone with Bruce yesterday

had filled her with a longing for more, made her realise even more surely, how she had missed his companionship during the recent weeks. Were those hours an earnest of a renewal of their earlier friendship, and if they were, was she going to be able to conceal her real feelings? There had been one episode yesterday which had ruffled the serenity of their new rapport. It had only been momentary but it had been there. It had occurred just before they pushed the boat into the water. Bruce had been showing her all its amenities.

'She's all fitted up for a cruise of several days,' he had said proudly, ushering her into the cabin. 'There's a small stove and a couple of bunks, and it is possible, if I want, to fit another bunk outside. Perhaps...' he stopped, flushing uncomfortably, 'we might all three have a night at sea later on.' The words came out in a rush, were obviously a cover-up for his original thought, and Beverley was sure that she knew what he had intended to say. He had meant to suggest that Beverley should join him in an overnight cruise. Then he had remembered, not only that Beverley was a woman, but that he was a married man.

The weather god did at last relent, and the day finally came when the suggested sail did materialise. Beverley's hopes that the trip might be for herself and Bruce alone were doomed to disappointment—she had not really expected it to be otherwise. From the time they started, Bruce kept her on her toes the whole time. Cora had received the news that Beverley was to crew with acclamation.

'Bruce tells me you are willing to crew for him,' she had said. 'Well, good luck to you. You are welcome to the job.' She seated herself by John Sheavyn who had already taken his place. 'We'll be content to be passengers, won't we, Mr. Sheavyn?'

'There's no option for me,' replied the old man. 'Though I would rather be sailing her any day.'

'Have you done a lot of sailing, Mr. Sheavyn?' asked Beverley.

'I should say I have. My father took me out when I was a tiny chap and I've been at it ever since. I taught Bruce here, didn't I, Bruce?'

'You did, Grandpa, and I couldn't have had a better teacher. I'm trying to pass it on to Beverley now, but she's a late starter. Are you ready to get on to that jib now, Beverley?'

'Aye, aye, sir,' laughed Beverley.

'You're getting the lingo already.' Cora eyed the girl narrowly. Was she feeling jealous, already regretting the relinquishment of the job she had professed to find so distasteful? wondered Beverley.

They got under way. Beverley, manipulating the jib, was the target for a stream of direction and information from the man at the helm. She fired her own questions too.

'Why do Mr. Sheavyn and Cora shift their places every time you tack?' she asked at one time.

'To maintain the balance of the boat,' Bruce explained. 'If they didn't she'd be too heavily weighted on their side and we would capsize.'

As they had tacked down the river they had been followed at quite close quarters by another yacht, manned by four young fellows. When they reached the open waters of the bay, they had expected to throw them off, not only expected but hoped. The young men were in exuberantly high spirits, their voices rent the air in a discordance of shouted pop numbers. For some unknown reason the young men had different ideas. They continued to steer a course close on the heels of the *Swallow*, as Bruce's yacht was named.

'Why the dickens can't they clear off?' asked Bruce irritably, voicing the thoughts of them all. 'Surely there's ample room for them. There might have been some excuse when we were in the river, but there's none now. I've half a mind to give them a hail and tell them to fish elsewhere.'

'They are not fishing, are they?' asked Beverley. She had seen no sign of fishing tackle.

'No, just a figure of speech,' laughed Bruce. 'Not part of your nautical education. But I think I will give them a call.' He lifted his hands to his mouth but his grandfather stopped him.

'Let them be, lad,' he advised. 'They're not doing us any harm.'

No, thought Beverley, they are not doing us any harm, but they are disturbing the peace, plastering with annoyance what should have been idyllic. The morning's early promise had been fulfilled. The sun shone from a sky whose blue was rendered all the more intense by the white clouds which scudded hurriedly across it. The early breeze had strengthened. Out in the bay it was distinctly choppy. Beverley found that she was enjoying today's choppiness even more than the comparative calm of the previous occasion. Those horrible pop songs were the only discordant note. If only they had sung sea shanties, she thought, it wouldn't have been so bad—though not one of the young men seemed to have any idea of tune. She wished that Mr. Sheavyn had been less tolerant, that he had let Bruce continue with his 'Halloo'. Later she was to remember this wish and to be thankful that it had not been granted.

'Like a change, Beverley? Like to take a turn at the tiller?' called Bruce after they had been sailing for the best part of an hour.

'Could I? I should like to try, but you don't think I'll upset you all, do you?'

'No reason why you should. Not if you do what you're told. Come on, change over.'

They changed places. Under Bruce's shouted instructions, Beverley managed, more or less successfully, to tack and to gybe, to turn into the wind, to run with the wind

'Hi! You'll have us all overboard,' Cora had cried at an early stage of the proceedings as the yacht dipped alarmingly to one side, but Bruce had quickly restored her confidence.

'That's nothing,' he had said. 'Carry on, Beverley. You're doing fine. I'll make a yachtsman of you in no time. What do you say, Grandpa?'

'She's shaping very well,' agreed the old man. 'Haven't you done any yachting before?' he asked Beverley.

'I've not even been in a rowing boat,' confessed Beverley.

'Then you're a natural,' said Bruce.

Bruce's words of praise warmed her inwardly. As she obeyed his every command she allowed her imagination to stray, visualising long hours spent in sailing with Bruce during the summer that lay ahead. She forgot for the moment what lay ahead. She forgot for the moment that she had decided that if Bruce did not send her packing when the library was finished that she herself must perform the same operation. She was brought back to reality with a bump. Her eyes had strayed in Bruce's direction just as she was hauling in the main sheet preparatory to tacking. She saw Cora move towards Mr. Sheavyn. As she watched the woman gave the old man a push, a push which dislodged him from his seat and sent him spinning into the water. In a flash Beverley was in after him. She did not hear Bruce's warning cry of 'gybe', did not see the boom swing across the deck, catching Cora on the head, sweeping her off the deck, but she did hear the splash.

Beverley was a skilled swimmer, had won her life-saving certificate at school. It was hardly a second's work to grab the old man, to tug him back to the yacht's side where Bruce was waiting to help them both aboard. The man himself was hardly yet aware of what had happened. He had had his back to the main part of the boat. His first indication of anything wrong had been when Beverley had omitted to swing the boom, when he had shouted 'gybe'. He had heard a splash,

242

another and then still another, all in such quick succession that they had been nearly simultaneous. He was about to jump in himself when he realised that two of the young fellows from the following yacht were also in the water. They, too, had gone to the rescue.

'What happened?' He was lifting his grandfather over the gunwale. Even as he spoke one of the young men had reached the side of the boat, holding Cora in his arms. Bruce stared at the inert figure of his wife in amazed consternation. He had not known that she too had gone over board. In the space of a few seconds the sea around the boat, so it seemed to him, had become alive with bodies. There had been five, he realised now. In almost a few seconds it was empty again. All the bodies were on the deck of his yacht.

'What happened?' he asked again as he knelt by his grandfather, working rhythmically to bring life back to the old man.

There was no reply to his question. Instead: 'This dame's a goner.' The words came from one of the young men who was bending over the woman he had pulled from the sea.

'She got what she asked for.' It was the second young man this time. 'Anyhow, who is she? Why should she push the old chap into the sea?'

'Push him into the sea!' Bruce Sheavyn

stopped his work and stared at the speaker. 'What do you mean?'

'What I say. The dame deliberately pushed the old fellow into the water. We both saw it, didn't we, Dave?' he appealed to his friend. He turned to Beverley. 'You saw it too, didn't you?' he asked. 'That's why you were so quick off the mark in jumping after him, wasn't it?'

'Yes.' The word had to be said though as she looked at Bruce's face Beverley felt that she would rather have done anything than add her confirmation to the young man's assertion.

'We'll talk about that later.' Bruce made a visible effort to speak normally. 'For now, let us get them down into the cabin. Can you help me with Grandfather, Beverley. He's coming round now.'

Between them they placed the sick old man on one of the bunks. His eyes were open now. He seemed about to ask a question.

'It's all right, Grandpa. There's been an accident, but you're all right now.'

'Cora, she pushed...' The enormity of what he was saying suddenly struck the old man. He could say no more.

'Yes, Grandpa. We know all about it.' But he did not know all about it. In spite of all the corroborative evidence he could not believe this horrifying fact. He looked across at the inanimate form on the other bunk. He ought to go across to her, to make sure that the young man was right, that she was really dead, but he felt that he could not touch her.

'Are you sure she's dead?' Had it been he who asked that question? The croaking voice was utterly unlike his own.

'Dead as mutton. She must have got a crack on the head from that boom. There's a great bump.' Both young men bent over what a few moments ago had been a living Cora. 'She's dead, right enough.' They straightened. 'Well, there's enough of us in this cabin, we'll get out. Want us to sail the yacht while you look after your grandfather?'

'Would you?' His gaze suddenly took in the dripping state of the two young men. Water ran from their shorts, from their sodden jerseys. 'No, you're soaking. Go and get changed. We'll manage.'

'Okay.' They started to leave the cabin, but 'Dave' turned back. 'Say what, we'll send one of the other chaps along. That'll free you.'

'Thank you.' Bruce accepted the offer gratefully. His grandfather needed immediate attention and not only was Beverley too much of a new hand to be trusted to run the boat single-handed, she would be useful here. He turned to her. 'Look in that locker,' he said, 'and see if you can find a towel and a pair of pyjamas.' He started to strip off his grandfather's sodden garments. 'Lucky I kept those here for just such an emergency. No, not such an emergency,' he said grimly. 'Thank you,' as Beverley handed him the things. 'Now, put the kettle on. Water in the bucket. Matches on that shelf. Put a pan on as well. We had better fill a hot-water bottle for grandfather.' He gave terse orders, telling her where to find everything, while he gently dried and rubbed the old man.

'Warm now, Grandpa?' he asked as he pulled the blankets up.

'Aye, I'm all right.' He spoke sleepily.

'Don't go to sleep just yet. Beverley is coming up with a mug of strong tea. Plenty of sugar,' he told her as she poured out the steaming liquid.

Beverley handed Bruce the mug, turned back to the stove to fill the hot-water bottle. Bruce lifted his grandfather to a sitting position and held the mug to his lips as he drank. In spite of his assertion that he was all right the old man's hands shook too much for him to manipulate the mug by himself.

'Make us a mug each, will you, Beverley?' asked Bruce when he had eased the old man down once more. 'I think we could both do with it.' He moved out of the cabin, keeping his eyes averted from the still figure on the other bunk. 'We'll drink it outside, shall we?'

They stood side by side, leaning against the cabin wall, sipping the hot, strong, sweet concoction. Normally Beverley would have thought it poisonous, but now she drank it gratefully. She shivered.

'What a fool I am!' Bruce Sheavyn suddenly became conscious of her as something other than a pair of ministering hands. 'I sent those chaps off to change and never gave you a thought. Just a second, I'll go and get you a towel and some dry togs and then you can slip into the cabin and change.' He dived into the cabin, returning in a few seconds. 'All yours,' he said. 'Grandpa's sleeping like a babe,' he did not mention the other silent figure, 'give yourself a jolly good rub.'

He was waiting for her when she came out in slacks and sweater, both sizes too large for her, but dry and warm. 'That's better,' he approved. 'Are you really warm now?' He did not wait for her answer, but went to the young man at the helm. 'Would you mind carrying on for a few more minutes?' he asked. 'I want to get things sorted out a bit.'

'That's okay by me. She's a beauty to sail.'

'By the way, why were you following us? What was the game?'

'No game. We're strangers to this part and we could see that you knew the waters so we thought we'd benefit from your knowledge.'

'As simple as that.'

'As simple as that. What had you been expecting me to say?'

'I don't know. I've been thinking up all sorts of things during these last few minutes.' He switched the subject. 'Were you like those other two chaps who came aboard? Did you see everything that happened?'

'Yes.'

'Would you mind telling me. I knew nothing until I saw all those bodies in the water. It all happened too quickly and my back was to it.'

'Well, it all started with that dame giving the old man a push which sent him overboard. Before you could say "knife" this young girl,' he indicated Beverley, 'was after him. It's my opinion she couldn't have been too surprised at what happened. She was too quick off the mark. The boat swerved as she let go the sail and, of course, the boom swung. The dame who started the party just stood stock still when she saw the girl jump. Guess she hadn't expected that. Anyhow, she never saw the boom and it caught her a cracker and swept her overboard. Sort of poetic justice as you might say. Can't think what you were doing with that sort on the boat.'

'She was my wife.'

'Oh, sorry.' The young man stood abashed.

His hands twisted nervously at the sail. 'Guess I'd better be making myself scarce after that bloomer.'

'You weren't to know. Anyhow, thank you, and your chums, for all your help. I'll carry on now.'

'Right, I'll give the others a hail.' The other yacht was still in the offing. As the young man called, it hove-to. As one of the other young men pulled the two boats together he jumped across to his own boat. 'I don't know whether you'll be in need of any witnesses,' he said, 'but if you do, we're staying several days more. Up the Silverdale Road.' He pulled a notebook out of his pocket and tearing out a sheet scribbled an address on it.

'Thank you.' Bruce took the sheet of paper and stuffed it in the pocket of his slacks. 'I'll get in touch with you if it is necessary.' He raised his hand in farewell as the other yacht drew away.

'Shall I take the jib?' Beverley moved towards the middle of the boat. It would be a relief to take the jib sail, to have her back turned to Bruce. He, however, decreed otherwise.

'No,' he said. 'I can manage and I think you have had as much as you should take today. You sit there. I haven't finished with questions yet, but first of all I must thank you for being so prompt to rescue my grandfather. I am afraid it might have gone hardly with him if you had not been "so quick off the mark", as that fellow said. But what did he mean when he said you were not unprepared?'

'I . . .' Beverley hesitated.

'I want to know.' It was not Bruce the friend, who was speaking now, it was Bruce Sheavyn, her employer. There was the hard note of authority. 'Had Cora done anything like that before?' he demanded.

'I . . .' once more she hesitated.

'Tell me,' he said again.

'Yes, several times.' If he wanted it he should have it. She told him everything, from the very first time when Cora had seized the wheel of the car and directed it against the old man. She told him of the open window.

'I suppose that time when she was late in picking him up at the office was a put-up job too,' he said slowly. 'Why didn't you tell me?' He turned on her suddenly. 'Why did you keep it to yourself? Surely you could see how great the danger was?'

'But you knew. You knew what Cora was up to.' The words came out with a rush, unbidden. As she had been talking the memory of that overheard conversation had thrust itself into her consciousness, springing from the depths into which she thought she

250

had successfully buried it.

'I—knew—what—Cora—was—up—to!'
Bruce stared at her as though he could not
have heard aright. 'What do you mean?' The
first words had barely dropped from his lips,
had come as slowly as the drops from a
measuring phial. These were rapped out with
the speed of gunshot.

'I heard you . . .' She could not go on.

'Never mind. We'll settle that later. But if
you recognised the danger and you could not
tell me, why didn't you tell somebody else?'

'I did. Matthew and Florence knew. We
were all on the watch.'

'Matthew and Florence knew as well, and
yet not one of you said a word to me! Did they
think I knew?'

'No, and I didn't really,' she ignored the
ironical smile. She knew she was telling the
truth in spite of that unlucky outburst. What
had made her blurt out that accusation, an
accusation which, even at the outset, she had
felt could not be warranted?

'How could we?' she cried. 'How could we
tell you that your wife was trying to murder
your grandfather? We had no actual proof. If
we had said anything Cora would have been
able to throw ridicule on the idea. You would
never have believed us.'

No, he would not; he could not have let

himself believe Cora capable of such a dastardly action, could not have faced, without the actual proof he now had, that his wife was a potential murderer. He had always known that Cora did not like his grandfather, had resented not only his presence, but also the fact that he still held so many of the reins in his own hands. He had realised lately that she was very discontented, that part of that discontent was rooted in the fact that her very real abilities had not sufficient outlet. Those smothered abilities had indeed taken bad ways and part of the guilt was his. He ought to have seen it earlier, and when he did see it he ought to have acted. There might still have been time to avert this if he had only acted when he first realised how things were.

'We're nearly in.' He had been so lost in his thoughts that Beverley feared he was steering blindly. It was quite a while since they had left the open water behind them. The land on their side was creeping nearer and nearer. The weather, too, had changed. The sun had vanished, heavy clouds rolled across the sky, the wind was more than fresh, it was distinctly strong. Beverley had had time to give a thought to that other yacht, to hope that the young fellows on it had had the sense to steer for home—they had only been indifferent yachtsmen. She had a warm feeling for them;

not only because they had come so willingly and cheerily to their help, but because their cognisance of what had happened had made her own task so much easier. How could she herself have told Bruce that his wife had pushed Mr. Sheavyn into the water? True, the old man had said that this was the case, but, unsupported, it might have been deemed to be just imagination; and it would not have been easy for her to say otherwise. They had smoothed her path in one direction, but there was nobody who would pave the way for the trouble which lay ahead.

Bruce had only by-passed the accusation which she had flung at him. The reckoning was to come later. At least there was going to be no opportunity for it now. Bruce was turning the yacht into the harbour.

George was waiting at the jetty. Bruce jumped out, said a few hurried words to the man. Beverley noted the shocked expression which overlay his earlier welcoming one. Bruce turned back on to the yacht, George followed him. Beverley stood, not knowing quite what part she should play in this tragic drama.

'Beverley, will you help me to get Grandfather to the car?'

'Aye, you do that, Mr. Bruce. And then go and phone the undertaker. I'll look after the

253

rest. You get the old gentleman home as fast as you can.'

Beverley followed Bruce into the cabin. John Sheavyn opened his eyes as they entered. On the other bunk lay a still form covered by a blanket. By common consent Bruce and Beverley both turned away from it.

'Can you get to the car, Grandpa, if Beverley and I go one each side of you?' He lifted the old man gently from the bunk, raised him to a standing position. Between them, Beverley and Bruce led him along the deck, across the connecting plank, over the stones, along the tiny promenade, to the car. He sank back into his seat with relief, but did not close his eyes again. Instead he seemed to be quite alert.

'Where's Cora?' he asked when Bruce had returned from telephoning.

'She's...' Bruce hesitated. Should he tell the old man now or leave it till later? 'She's dead,' he said finally. 'She tumbled overboard after being knocked by the boom.'

'She pushed me over, you know.' John Sheavyn spoke quietly but very definitely. The fact that Cora was dead appeared to make less impression than his knowledge that she had tried to drown him.

Once more Bruce hesitated. There would be no possibility of deceiving his grandfather

254

as to what had really happened.

'Yes, I know. Grandfather,' he came to a sudden decision. 'Do you think we could keep that fact secret? Need we say anything at the inquest? Do you think we could keep quiet about that, but tell everything else as it really happened. What need is there to blacken Cora's character after her death?'

'None, I should say,' agreed the old man. He turned round to the back of the car where Beverley was seated. 'What do you say, Beverley?'

'I think so, too, but those young men know otherwise,' she reminded Bruce.

'What other young men?'

'Some fellows on another yacht, who came to our rescue, Grandpa. They saw everything. I'll go and see them later. I'm sure they won't make any trouble.'

They reached the house. 'Call Matthew, will you, Beverley?' said Bruce. 'And don't say anything,' he warned.

As if she would have done, thought Beverley, but she did wonder how much Matthew and his wife guessed as they listened to Bruce's account of the 'accident'.

CHAPTER FOURTEEN

Apart from the staff and Gilbert Marrow, Bruce was the only one from Willerton Grange who went to Cora Sheavyn's funeral. The doctor had been called in to John Sheavyn immediately after his return to the house on that fateful afternoon. He had decreed that the old man should spend several days in bed, saying that he would return the next day. He then found he had two patients, for Florence had insisted that he should be brought in to Beverley. The latter had spent a restless night, tossing and turning from side to side. Time after time she had reversed her pillow, hoping in vain to find a cool spot. She had slept intermittently, only to find herself waking up bathed in perspiration, struggling with the aftermath of some nightmarish dream. Sometimes she was fighting Cora, trying to prevent her from pushing John Sheavyn deeper and deeper into the water. At other times it was she herself whom Cora was pushing back into the sea, knocking her hands off the gunwale as she tried to get a grip. Yet again she would find herself in the water, trying to tow Cora's dead body to the yacht. Always Cora was there, dead or alive, but always wearing that smile of malicious triumph which she had glimpsed at the moment before she herself jumped in the sea after John Sheavyn. She did manage to get a few hours' sleep as daylight came, but when she awoke she felt drugged and heavy. There was no jumping out of bed, no running to the window as she had done yesterday. It took her all her time to make herself get out of bed and the task of dressing took every ounce of energy.

'Well, you look as though you've had a night on the tiles.' Florence came bustling in with her breakfast tray. She had decided to take on Matthew's duties this morning, thinking she would glean more information as to yesterday's doings than would her husband, but one glance at Beverley's face told her that she was not going to be any more lucky here than she had been with her master. 'You do look bad,' she put her hand on Beverley's forehead. 'You are hot!' she exclaimed. 'It's in bed, you ought to be, young lady, and, unless I'm mistaken, you won't be wanting this breakfast.'

'No,' agreed Beverley. The very sight of the heavily laden tray with its steaming bacon and eggs had filled her with nausea.

'You sit there a minute while I make your bed, and then you're going to get straight back

257

into it, and I'll bring you a hot lemon.' She hurriedly remade the bed, talking as she did so. 'It strikes me you got it worse than the master. He's as chirpy as a cricket this morning, wants to get up, but the doctor says as he's got to stay there, certainly over the weekend. I'll get the doctor to come and see you when he comes.'

'It's all right. I don't need him,' protested Beverley. 'It's only a bit of a chill.'

'Bit of a chill or not, you're going to have him,' said Florence firmly.

The doctor certainly diagnosed a chill, but a serious one. He had insisted that Beverley would need several days at least in bed, and the girl found that she was only too willing that it should be so. Those days in bed gave her leisure to think, to plan her coming explanation to Bruce Sheavyn, but they were a mixed blessing since they also gave her time to anticipate his reaction.

Why had she been such a fool? Why had she accused Bruce of knowing about Cora's activities when she did not even believe it? Would she never learn? She had thought these last months had done something for her, given her a deeper knowledge into human relationships, but she began to doubt it. Given a report on that subject, she thought, she would still rate an E, the failure mark, and the

258

failure mattered more than ever now since she had learned the meaning of love. If there had ever been the slightest possibility of Bruce loving her, she had scotched it most effectively.

She only saw Bruce once before the funeral and then only for a few minutes. He came into her room for a few minutes on the Sunday evening.

'I've been to see those fellows,' he told her, after he had enquired as to how she was feeling. 'They agreed with me that no purpose was to be served by telling how my grandfather came to fall into the water. They are coming to the inquest and will give a full account of it all except for that one thing. They were very decent.'

'I'm glad,' said Beverley. 'It will make things that much easier.' Not that anything was very easy for Bruce at the moment, she thought. The experience had taken its toll of him. He might not be in bed with a temperature, but he looked drawn and haggard.

'You have not said anything to Matthew or Florence, have you?' He looked at her searchingly. 'I'm sorry,' as she flushed up, 'I ought to know that you would not have done, but Florence is not easy to put off. She has been full of the "I know more than I'm saying" attitude, and I'm pretty sure she thinks everything was not so straightforward as I pretend.'

'Yes, she's been like that with me, and it has been rather hard because she knows what has happened before. She's done all she could, short of asking outright, to find out how things happened, but I've been a clam.'

'Yes, and I expect that the very fact that you have been such a clam has added fuel to her suspicions. Not that she or Matthew would tell anyone else if they did know, but I would rather they didn't. I can't help their suspicions, but I can prevent the certainty.'

He did not stay many more seconds, nor did he mention Beverley's own accusations. She was right when she suspicioned that he had enough on his plate at present without piling it with further disputatious matter.

On the day of the funeral she was allowed up for the first time. She sat at her window and watched the funeral cortège leave. Bruce and Gilbert Marrow were in the first car. Matthew and Florence, in heavy black, were in the second car. Beverley could not name the occupants of the other cars. She could not help wondering what were the real feelings of the occupants of that second car, what thoughts were masked by the solemn visages which they had donned to be in keeping with the funeral garments which country usage decreed? She had no doubt that they would be at complete variance with the outward trappings.

'I suppose I oughtn't to say it,' Florence had said to her only that morning, 'but however it happened, it's good riddance to bad rubbish, and you know that's the truth, Miss Beverley.'

Yes, it is the truth, the girl had thought, but she had not said the words aloud. Now that there was no longer any need for the help of these two friends, a feeling of loyalty to Bruce blocked any display of whole-hearted agreement with their strictures on his late wife, and the blockage was the more concrete since she was also forced to hide from them her knowledge that these strictures were more than warranted.

She could not help thinking how sad it was that there should be nobody at the funeral except Gilbert who really cared about Cora. Those other mourners were mere acquaintances, in general paying their respects to one who had been the wife of the heir to Willerton Grange. Cora had made no real friends in the district. As for Bruce, what could his feelings be? Whatever they were, they could not be the normal ones of a young man following his wife to her grave.

Bruce's thoughts as he drove through the dripping countryside—it had rained all

morning and the sky was still heavily grey—
were almost nil. During these last days, he had
struggled and fought with the heavy
depression which threatened to overwhelm
him. He had been deeply shocked by
Beverley's revelations, blamed himself that
such things could have been. He had delved
deeply into the past, trying to discover where
he, himself, had gone wrong. Had he been an
adequate husband, he reasoned, Cora could
not have come to this, yet as he tortured
himself, he knew that the true blame was not
altogether his, that the evil must have been in
Cora long before he knew her. Perhaps had
she married differently those roots might
never have sprouted, but there he could not
blame himself, for as he had long realised, it
had been Cora who had done the wooing. As
he pondered and pondered he came to the
conclusion that it would have needed an older
and more brutal man to have kept Cora on an
even keel. Where he had failed was in not
realising her boredom, in not providing her
with the means of using her abilities, in
thinking that she could find content in a quiet
existence. He wondered why she had not
openly rebelled, why she had not insisted in
living her own life—he did not know that
having tried this she wanted more, that
ambition denigrated the past, poisoned the

present.

As he had wrestled he had known that he must lay Cora's ghost and he had finally done so. Those three days he spent in spirit with his dead wife, conscious that though she had forfeited much, he still had a debt to her. Love had flown long before the final horror, but before he could start on a new life, he must pay to her whatever debt he owed. As he turned from the newly made grave he knew that in that grave he had buried not only his wife, but also, as far as was humanly possible, all the memories and regrets of those last years which had culminated so tragically. It was to the future that he intended to look now, a future which undoubtedly held problems, but they were problems which he was convinced were such as he should be able to solve.

Though he had never had very much sympathy with his brother-in-law, Bruce Sheavyn was well aware that Cora's death would be a shattering blow to Gilbert Marrow, and he had hoped—and believed—that Gilbert might never know the real circumstances of his sister's death, that his sorrow might not have to be commingled with the bitterness which his cognisance of her true character must inevitably bring. Through no fault of his sister's husband, Gilbert did learn that there was more to the accident than he had been told. He had arrived at Willerton Grange in time for the inquest and had accompanied Bruce to the little schoolroom in which it took place. It was on the way out that he overheard the scraps of a conversation which made him demand an explanation from Bruce. The latter had stayed behind to speak to the coroner.

'You go on,' he had said. 'I'll catch you up in a minute.' Gilbert was still in the school playground when sentences, spoken just behind him, arrested his attention.

'Well, that dame certainly got off light. It looks as though nobody but her husband and that girl—besides us—will ever know what actually happened.'

What really happened! It took all the will-power Gilbert Marrow possessed to prevent him from turning round, but the thought that he might hear more kept his head in its original position, slowed his footsteps.

'It's a case of "The evil was interred with her bones". Isn't that *Julius Caesar* or something? I seem to remember something of the sort from School Cert. days.'

'Yes.' There was a hoot of laughter, quickly stifled. 'Only you've got it all wrong. It's "the evil that men do lives after them, the good is oft interred with their bones".'

'Oh, well, you always were the brainy one,

Dave, but my version's the right one for this dame. She's got away with it.'

'Sh! Somebody might hear and we did promise not to say anything.' The last speaker embarked on a more innocuous subject. Gilbert turned round as he reached the gate. Immediately behind him were the four young men who had corroborated Bruce's account of the incident. Gilbert tackled Bruce as soon as they got into the house.

'What exactly did happen on that boat?' he asked. He told what he had overheard.

'I didn't exactly see,' prevaricated Bruce. He was extremely loth to tell Cora's brother such damning truths about his sister.

'But you know what happened.'

'Look here, Gilbert, suppose you ask Beverley about it. She saw everything.' And all that went before, he told himself. I am passing the buck to Beverley, he reflected, but she is not so close to it all as I am. She will probably make a better job of telling Gilbert than I should.

That afternoon, Gilbert went up to Beverley's room.

'Bruce sent me to you,' he explained after the first civilities. 'I want to know just what happened on that boat.' He once more retailed the young men's conversation. As Bruce had done, so did Beverley. She tried to hedge.

'It's best forgotten, Gilbert,' she said. 'It was all a horrible muddle.'

Gilbert was not to be put off. He insisted on being told everything. Beverley would not have thought him capable of such insistence. There was more to Gilbert than she had thought. Once more she told herself how little she knew about human nature, how much she had to learn.

'That wasn't the first time, was it?' he said when she had finished.

'How do you know?' Beverley stared at him. It was not a question, it was an assertion.

'From things she said last Easter. I was afraid. I warned her that, apart from anything else, if anything did happen to the old man and Bruce guessed it had had anything at all to do with her he would never forgive her.'

'What did she say?' Beverley was quick on to this. Gilbert's answer to her query might have the power to disperse every doubt of Bruce that could possibly lurk in her mind. She had told herself over and over again that she was quite convinced, but a denial from Cora would give her complete surety, complete peace of mind.

'She said that she was well aware of that, but that she had got all her wits about her and she would make quite sure that he would never guess. I begged her to put the whole thing out

266

of her mind, used every argument I knew, moral and otherwise. I thought I had succeeded, but I might have known, that I should never be able to convince her that I knew better than she did. I was always the little brother to her, to be guided, not to guide.'

'But didn't you point out to her that it was murder?' That aspect seemed to have been completely overlooked.

'Of course I did, but I knew that if Cora had decided on a certain course, the name—and its implications—would mean nothing to her. She would already have weighed that up. The trouble is,' he sighed, 'our parents mixed us up at birth.'

'How could they?' Seeing that there was more than a dozen years difference between them, Beverley could not see any sense in the statement.

'I don't mean literally. I mean that Cora should have been the man and I the woman. We should both have been much better people then.'

He stayed and talked a while longer, dragging from Beverley all that she had previously told Bruce. By the time he left the girl discovered that she had a far greater respect for Gilbert Marrow than she would ever have thought possible from her earlier acquaintance with him. She was quite sorry that he was going back immediately after the funeral and that was not only because she would have been thankful for somebody to act as a buffer between herself and Bruce when they resumed normal relations.

Bruce had not lived in his own apartments since Cora's death. He felt that he could hardly bring himself to enter them. They had always been to a certain extent alien to him. Cora's attitude to the old house and its decoration had been so different from his, but it now not only shouted Cora at him, but it underlined all their differences. He slept in one of the guest rooms, used the library as his sitting-room. It was to the library that he summoned Beverley just a week after the tragically eventful sail.

'Will you ask Miss Beverley to come to the library?' he had asked Matthew after lunch. He had only seen the girl once since that day. On the day following the funeral he had returned to business and had not arrived home until the evening when he had made no attempt to get in touch with her.

'In the library, Matthew?' Beverley wished she could have asked the old man how his master looked, whether his face when he gave the message had been stern and set. She had been waiting and waiting for such a message, had even wondered as the days went by, and it did not come, whether she should take the initiative and go herself to see Bruce. She was now pretty well recovered, but had kept to her own rooms, apart from an occasional visit to John Sheavyn who was now nearly well though the doctor insisted on keeping him very quiet.

'Hello, Beverley, come and sit by the fire.' Bruce drew a chair close to the hearth. It was so like that first time when she had come to Willerton Grange just about six months ago, and yet so different. Cora had been there then. Cora was dead now. Then she had been at the beginning of her time here. Now, she told herself, she was at the end. 'Are you feeling quite fit again now?' he asked her.

'Yes, thank you.' And ready to start work again, she would have liked to say, but those words were not for her. If they were to be said at all they must come from the man sitting in the chair on the opposite side of the fireplace, but he did not say them. Instead, he said:

'I think you owe me an explanation, Beverley.'

'Yes. Yes, I do.' It had come now. In spite of all her preparation for this moment she found herself at a loss. 'I'm sorry, Bruce. I . . .'

'Yes?' He did not help her. He just sat and

waited. A coal dropped from the fire. He leant forward, picked up the tongs, replaced the coal. Still he waited.

'What made you say that I knew what Cora was doing?' he said finally.

'I heard you. Twice.'

'Heard me? What do you mean? When on earth did you hear me say that I knew that my wife was trying to murder my grandfather?' He looked as though he was holding himself in, perhaps, thought Beverley, asking for patience to deal with this mad woman.

'N-not in so many words,' she faltered, 'but it all seemed to add up. And yet I was sure it couldn't be true,' she hastened to add, sensing that she was only making matters worse.

'Suppose you begin at the beginning,' suggested Bruce. 'You say there were two occasions. What was the first and what did I actually say?'

'It was on the day I arrived.' Given a lead Beverley found herself able to carry on. 'I was just going to knock at the library door when I heard Cora's voice. She seemed very angry.'

'What did she say?'

'She said, "I'll kill him myself if you don't get a move on," and you said, "I tell you I will, but in my own time."'

'And you thought that meant we were planning to murder my grandfather?'

270

'Not really. I couldn't think what it was at first. Then I thought it might be a dog or a horse perhaps, and I tried to find out but you said you had not got a dog and only one horse which you showed me.' Beverley had gone over this so many times that there was no necessity for her to think, to choose her words.

Bruce had been looking at her in puzzlement from the moment when she had told him of the actual words she had overheard. Now his face cleared.

'I've got it,' he said. 'We had a dog, but he was very old and incurably ill. I knew that I ought to put him out of his misery but I had not been able to make myself do so. I remember now that it was on the night that you arrived that I finally brought myself to do it. Does that satisfy you?'

'Yes, but I don't need satisfying. Gilbert . . .'

'Oh! What has Gilbert to do with it?'

'He told me after the inquest that he knew that Cora was plotting something. He tried to dissuade her by telling her that if you ever suspected anything it would put paid to all her hopes.'

'Another person who knew! Well, I'm not satisfied yet, even if you are. What was the second occasion?'

'It was just before Easter.' Beverley

blushed, wished that she could find some way of wriggling out of this, but Bruce sat there as though carved in stone, waiting. 'You were just coming out of your grandfather's room,' she said, 'and Cora met you and asked, "Well, what did he say?" I had just opened the library door to go up to my room, but when I heard that I stopped. You see,' she excused herself, 'I already knew that Cora had twice tried to kill Mr. Sheavyn and I had to know if this was another threat. I had to, hadn't I?' she pleaded.

'Yes. Go on.'

'I listened. You said "Nothing much, he hadn't any idea," or something of that sort. Then Cora said, "Well, that's it then. I warn you, Bruce," I can remember the exact words, "I'm going to stop at nothing if that man doesn't go, and he knows it too. I've shown him that already."'

'So you thought I was in agreement with Cora's "stop at nothing" where my grandfather was concerned. Couldn't you see that I loved my grandfather, Beverley?'

'Yes, of course I could, and I just didn't see how it could be true, but it all tied up so. I didn't really believe it. I kept telling myself so, but it was always at the back of my mind and it just hopped out that day on the boat.'

'I'll say it did,' said Bruce grimly. 'Once

more, I have got a simple explanation. Cora was very worried about Gilbert's friendship with the new partner they had taken on. She still had a number of shares in the firm and was determined to use her influence. She asked me to ask Grandfather how she could do it. She had already sent several threatening letters.'

'Oh.' Beverley digested this. 'I didn't know that, of course, but I did know that Cora wanted Mr. Sheavyn out of the way.'

'Yes, I suppose it was a natural conclusion, but you can't have had a very high opinion of me.'

'I have. I . . .' She bit back the next words just in time.

'Yes,' Bruce cocked his head.

'I always have,' she improvised.

'That wasn't what you were going to say,' he accused. 'What were you going to say?' he asked quietly.

She turned away, gazed at the window, beyond which the rain fell relentlessly on an already soaked earth. Since that one good day, the day which had ended so tragically, there had not been a single day when it had not rained, weeping, but surely not for Cora she thought now. 'Stop being fanciful.' The words were only in her mind. Her next spoken words must be an answer to Bruce's question and she knew that she was deliberately turning her mind away from that answer. How could a girl tell a man that she loved him when he did not love her? But Bruce still waited.

'I love you,' she whispered at last. It was as though he had dragged the words out of her. The effect was electric. In a matter of seconds she was out of her chair and sitting on his knee; by what agency she would have found it hard to say, but she could have sworn it was not her own.

'And I love you,' he said between his kisses. These stopped abruptly. 'But are you quite sure that I am not a murderer?' he asked. 'Because you would not want to marry a murderer, would you?' Her protestations were drowned by a renewed onslaught of kisses. 'You know, love,' he said when the next breathing space occurred, 'What I ought to do after the way you have behaved is to have you across my knee the other way.'

There flew into her memory those similar words uttered by Mr. Pemberton in what seemed another life. Then she had been filled with terrified horror. Now she gave a happy chuckle and snuggled closer.

'I take it then that you are quite willing to become Mrs. Bruce Sheavyn. In spite of everything?'

'In spite of everything.' She giggled happily. 'But we can't announce it yet, Bruce.'

She sat up, suddenly serious, suddenly conscious that it was only a week since Bruce had been married to another woman, that it was only a week since Cora had died so tragically, and already she was contemplating marrying Cora's husband.

'Of course not. We must let an interval elapse.' He did not try to pretend that it was anything but convention that made that interval necessary. 'And we have a lot of planning to do.'

They talked and planned spasmodically. They were both too much overcome with the joy and freshness of their love for it to be more than spasmodic. There had to be interludes when the ecstasy of this new-found happiness submerged all else. It was during one of these intervals that there was a knock at the library door. Beverley sat up quickly, but not quickly enough. The knock and the appearance of Matthew's head were almost simultaneous. Bruce was the first to recover.

'It's all right, Matthew.' He smiled at the old man's dumbfounded expression. 'Miss Beverley and I are going to be married, but of course it is not going to be made public yet.'

'No, sir.' Matthew recovered his normal poise. 'I congratulate you both. I'm very glad, I'm sure. I just came to say . . .' He delivered his message with less than his usual formality.

He was too agog to return to the kitchen, to apprise his wife of the latest development.

'Eh, well, I'm not surprised.' Florence received the news with more calm than her husband had expected. 'If I'd only known I reckon I could have seen it coming long ago.'

'But you didn't.' Matthew was too used to his wife even to register, far less quarrel with, the illogicality of this statement.

'No, I didn't, but I can tell you one thing for sure. Just as nobody could abide the first, they're all going to love the second Mrs. Bruce.' She lifted the kettle from the stove and filled the silver teapot. 'You'd better take that tray in now,' she told her husband. She had been busy all the time she had been talking. 'And just don't go blundering in as soon as you've knocked,' she warned him. 'Give them time to sort themselves out.'